W   k-
tra   he
co   ro
Sa   nd
as   s.
Be   ut
an   ne
ma   ut
no   id
to   r.
B   ● 12/95   t
n   ●3/96   s
to   s
fa

Other Large Print Books
by Leslie Ernenwein

GUNFIGHTER'S RETURN
BULLET BARRICADE

SAVAGE JUSTICE

Leslie Ernenwein

Curley Publishing, Inc.
South Yarmouth, Ma.

Library of Congress Cataloging-in-Publication Data

Ernenwein, Leslie.
  Savage justice / Leslie Ernenwein.
     p.   cm.
  I. Title.
  [PS3555.R58S28   1992]
  813'.54—dc20
  ISBN 0–7927–0854–7 (hardcover : lg. print)   91–23830
  ISBN 0–7927–0855–5 (softcover : lg. print)   CIP

Published in Large Print by arrangement with Donald MacCampbell, Inc. in the United States and Canada.

Printed in Great Britain

SAVAGE JUSTICE

CHAPTER ONE

They were a strange trio, these three who halted dust-peppered broncs on the rim-rock above Apache Tank. They were entirely dissimilar in face and form, yet they were marked by one common brand—the renegade brand of the gunsmoke breed.

Lee Beauregarde was the youngest of the three, and the tallest. His gray eyes were like steel slots against the 'dobe brown of his high-boned cheeks, and they showed scant interest in the town on the flats below. 'So that's Apache Tank,' he reflected, and thereafter gave his attention to shaping up a cigarette.

'That's her,' Red Valentine announced, his scarred, blocky face breaking into a grin. 'And she's the richest little town in this end of Arizony!'

'Wonder what kind of whiskey they sell down there,' Faro Savoy speculated in a voice that rasped like a rusty hinge. His black eyes were bright in their shadowed sockets, and twin stains of scarlet gave his chalky cheeks a rouged appearance. Thin to the point of emaciation, he looked like a man living on borrowed time. He said complainingly, 'That Lordsburg likker liked to've killed me.'

Lee Beauregarde lit his cigarette, breaking

1

the match as was dry-country custom before discarding it. He exhaled a deep drag of smoke and glanced casually at Savoy's disease-ravaged face. 'Any kind of whiskey is poison to you,' he drawled. 'Bugs and booze don't mix.'

Hair-trigger temper flamed in Savoy's feverish eyes. 'Save your goddam advice for them that wants it!' he croaked, and tried to smother the hacking cough that shook his reedy frame.

Red Valentine chuckled. 'You galoots got no imagination,' he jeered, and poked a stubby thumb toward the distance-hazed hills which formed Panamint Valley's western barrier. 'Look at all that there range just awaitin' to be took over by one strong outfit. We're due to git filthy rich in this country, and you're augerin' over whiskey!'

A skeptical smile twisted Beauregarde's lips. 'What makes you so sure there's easy money around here?' he asked. 'Apache Tank looks like just another wide place in the stage road to me.'

The red-haired rider said, 'I got it in black and white—a letter from a friend.'

'Didn't know you could read,' Beauregarde drawled. 'What's your friend's name?'

Valentine pulled a dog-eared envelope from his hip pocket and briefly scanned its return address. 'Strebor,' he reported. 'Sid Strebor. I knew him by a different name when he didn't have a plugged peso. Now he owns Skillet, the largest spread in this whole damn valley. Says he'll pay us top gun wages with a bonus to boot if we help him bust the Panamint Pool.'

A jackrabbit hopped from behind a boulder and paused to eye the three riders in trembling astonishment. Whereupon Red Valentine snatched up his gun, knocked the rabbit down with his first shot and proceeded to riddle the fluffy carcass with two additional slugs.

Beauregarde said, 'You like the feel of killing, don't you, Red?'

Valentine chuckled and reloaded his gun. 'A gink has got to keep his hand in,' he said, then peered questioningly at Beauregarde. 'Say, Feller—you had a gun rep back in Texas, but I ain't never seen you do no practicing. How come!'

Abruptly then Beauregarde was aware of the way Valentine and Savoy were watching him as if they were doubting his gunslick reputation. Their eyes held the meat glare of hungry wolves, and in that hushed instant Lee Beauregarde understood how tough a team he'd joined back there in New Mexico. These two weren't just saddle-tramp smokeroos taking a look-see over the hill; they belonged to the grisly brotherhood that kills for the sheer joy of killing . . .

'Got all the practice in the Lincoln County

3

fracas I'll ever need,' Beauregarde muttered.

They eyed him for a moment longer; then Savoy said, 'Let's git to a saloon before I choke to death.'

'Yeah,' Valentine agreed, 'I could do with some panther sweat myself. Mebbe they got percentage gals down there, like in Tombstone.'

They rode down the steep slope and were crossing the flats east of Apache Tank when Beauregarde noticed a rider approaching on a trail that angled into the stage road farther on. Something about the rider plucked at his interest, but it wasn't anything he could identify, and so he dismissed the rider from his thoughts . . .

When they were almost to the trail fork, Valentine said, 'There's a nice target, Lee—let's see you knock down that burro yonder.'

Beauregarde glanced at the browsing burro and shook his head.

Whereupon Faro Savoy said accusingly, 'You're goddam stingy with your lead. What you savin' it for?'

And Red Valentine asked, 'That Lincoln County doin's wouldn't've made you a gun shy, would it, Lee?'

Irritation touched Beauregarde's face and changed it. A v-shaped scar on his left cheek showed gray against the deepening color of his face; the angular line of his jaws grew sharper and his eyes turned a smoky blue. He said, 'There's a way you could find out—if you've got to know.'

For a hushed instant Valentine's muddy eyes held the shrewd squint of a man making a swift decision. Then his flat lips loosened into a lopsided grin and he said, 'No need to git proddy, *amigo*. I was just curious to see you toss a shot at a target, is all.'

'The burro might belong to someone in town,' Beauregarde muttered. 'Leastwise it don't belong to me.'

'Finders keepers,' Valentine declared and, lifting his gun, snapped three fast slugs into the animal before it collapsed. 'Now it's carryin' my personal brand,' he announced, 'the Three Bullet Brand!'

Which was when Beauregarde heard a voice call, 'You miserable killer!'

It was a rich contralto voice, and even as Beauregarde turned to look, he knew why that oncoming rider had plucked at his interest. The rider was a young woman—a tall, blonde-haired young woman with an oval face and the bluest eyes he had ever seen . . .

Those eyes were flashing now. They were filled with scorn, and she stared at Red Valentine as if seeing something repulsive; something utterly loathsome.

'You miserable killer!' she said again.

5

Valentine cuffed back his battered hat. 'A she-male—and purtier'n a litter o' spotted pups!' he blurted admiringly.

Faro Savoy's ghoulish face showed no interest at all. 'I'll still take whiskey,' he said sourly.

Beauregarde watched the girl ride up to Valentine. She wore a man's cotton shirt, Levi's and cowboy boots, and that rough attire somehow accentuated her full-blown beauty. Seeing the way her breasts rose and fell in rhythm to her excited breathing, Beauregarde recalled how long a time it had been since he'd seen a proud and proper girl.

There was an unflinching assurance in her eyes now as she faced Red Valentine. 'Why did you do it!' she demanded arrogantly.

Valentine brazenly ogled her supple body. 'I was just funnin' with my friends—to see who could shoot the fastest,' he explained.

'Fine fun!' she said scathingly. 'That burro was a little boy's pet!'

Red Valentine continued to smile in his smirking way. He kneed his horse over closer to the girl and said, 'Mebbe I'll give the boy two-three burros, girlie—if you'll ask me real nice.'

Faro Savoy winked at Beauregarde, and said amusedly, 'God's gift to wimmin goes into action agin.'

But Lee Beauregarde wasn't listening. He

6

was riding between Valentine and the girl. 'Leave her be,' he said flatly.

'What's the deal?' Valentine demanded. 'Who asked you in?'

'She's not your kind,' Beauregarde muttered, and narrowly watched quick resentment flare in Valentine's eyes.

'I like all kinds!' the redhead insisted. 'Tall or short, thick or thin, just so's they're purty in the face.'

Beauregarde's right hand nudged his gun loose from its greased leather, this instinctive gesture plainly showing how his thoughts were shaping. His long lips pressed into a straight, hard line that turned his face entirely bleak. But when he spoke his voice was low and quiet, almost friendly. 'Mebbe so, Red. Mebbe so. But don't mess with this kind. They got no more warmth than winter sun on a snowdrift.'

That drawling declaration seemed to baffle Valentine. His eyes squinted questioningly and some of the resentment ebbed out of them.

'The tall Texican knows his wimmin,' Savoy jeered, and went into another fit of coughing.

Beauregarde turned to the girl. For a moment they sat silently regarding each other, and in this suspended interval Lee Beauregarde reconstructed his first impression of her. She was proud and self-assured and a trifle arrogant. But she wasn't cold and she wasn't haughty. Her eyes held a searching frankness he had never seen in the eyes of a woman; he sensed a warmth and a sweetness in them that revived impulses long discarded . . .

Yet even then, even with some magnetic strand of her rich womanliness disrupting the orderly run of his thoughts, Lee Beauregarde didn't smile. And his voice showed no more than a frugal courtesy when he said, 'You'd better ride on, ma'am.'

She studied him with a steady and prolonged attention. There was perplexity in her questioning eyes, a frowning gravity on her full ripe lips. She said finally, 'I ride as I please, Mister—?'

'Beauregarde,' he offered. 'Lee Beauregarde.'

A mocking note came into her voice then. She said, 'Your description of my kind of girl is highly interesting, Mister Beauregarde. Especially coming from your kind of man—or should I say your kind of *killer*?'

The way she spoke that last word, putting a deliberate smear of condemnation on it, whipped up a quick resentment in Lee Beauregarde. *Who the hell does she think she's talking to?* he asked himself. But almost at once he realized she had sufficient reason for misjudging him, for thinking he was daubed with the same bloody brand as Valentine and Savoy. And as his resentment vanished he felt a queerly urgent regret. For a reason he couldn't

8

understand he had a desire to tell this girl that he hadn't chosen the gunslick game—that the death of his father had turned him into a back-trail saddle tramp . . .

But almost at once he stomped that impulse down, and grinning in the devil-be-damned manner of a rash smokeroo, said drawlingly, 'You've got a right to your opinions, ma'am. So have I.'

Abruptly then she touched spurs to her horse and rode on down the stage road at a run.

'You've got a hell of a way with wimmin!' Red Valentine scoffed.

He pointed to a triple-tracked scar on his temple. 'See that? A Mex gal did it with her fingernails. She had the longest nails and the slickest shape you ever saw on a female woman. By God, she was built like a brick smokehouse and full of fire. Well, after I kissed her a couple times she quit scratchin' and we had us a real nice time.'

Beauregarde watched the girl ride into town. He wondered what her name was, and why she was riding alone. A girl shouldn't be gadding around a country that was all primed for range war; not a girl who made a man's mind play tricks on him.

'Them fancy ones ain't no different from the others,' Valentine announced. 'They like a little sweetenin' now and then.'

9

Whereupon Faro Savoy rasped impatiently, 'To hell with all kinds of calico. I want a drink!'

★   ★   ★

Sheriff Sam Derbyshire sat in front of the Apache Tank jail, chewing tobacco with the methodical thoroughness of a mossyhorn steer. His angular, weather-honed face showed no sign of worry; he looked like a contented old man at peace with the world. But he wasn't . . .

Sam Derbyshire had been sheriff for ten consecutive terms and he took an honest pride in that record. Lately, though, the law badge on his vest had become a ponderous burden, and it grew heavier with each day's passing. Trouble was brewing all across the range; impending conflict threatened to turn Panamint Valley into a bloody bullring of death and destruction, and there was nothing he could do to stop it. For, according to Sam's code, a lawman had to abide by his oath of office. He couldn't take sides, no matter where his sympathies lay.

Now, as he watched Susan Blake ride her highstepping bay mare down Main Street, Sheriff Derbyshire remembered the days when this proud daughter of David Blake had come to town sitting on the sprung seat of a ranch wagon beside her father—a leggy, freckle-faced kid with bright ribbons in her hair. It occurred to him that she rode like her father, straight up in saddle; and she had Dave's direct way about her. But she possessed her mother's good looks, and because Sheriff Sam could recall a time when another Susan Blake had been the belle of Panamint Valley, he felt suddenly old and regretful. That other Susan had died giving this Susan birth . . .

When the girl halted in front of him, Sheriff Derbyshire shifted the tobacco bulge to his toothless right cheek and said, 'In town kind of early, ain't you, Susie?'

'Took a short cut,' she explained. 'Dad is bringing the wagon in for supplies.'

Then she said angrily, 'I just met three strangers out on the stage road, Sam. One of them killed Fonso Chacon's burro—for fun?'

'So?' Derbyshire commented, and peered down Main Street's patina of hoof-churned dust. 'That them comin' yonderly?'

Susan nodded, and said, 'They've got all the earmarks of professional gunslingers, Sam, I'll bet a yearling steer to a paper of pins that they're signing on with the Skillet. You should send them packing back the way they came!'

A sly twinkle warmed Derbyshire's cavernous eyes. 'Should I tell 'em the queen of Apache Tank commands them to be gone with utmost dispatch?' he asked

11

mischievously. 'Or shall I threaten to sick the White Knight of the Boxed P onto 'em?'

'Oh, Sam! Can't you see I've grown up?' she chided, tempering that demand with a thinly controlled smile. 'I'm not a kid, and Cliff Paddock isn't a White Knight. He's a hardworking young cowman who happens to want me for a wife.'

Derbyshire said soberly, 'Yes, you've grown up, Susie. And I've grown old—old enough to admit a sheriff ain't the all-powerful Knight of the Star you used to think he was. I can't order them strangers out of town just because you figger they're going to hire on with the Skillet, honey. And I can't take sides in this thing when the break comes. I hope you and Dave will understand that.'

'But it was Pool members who elected you last time, Sam. I don't see why you shouldn't stand by the men who've kept you in office all these years.'

The sheriff's wrinkled old face went hard; hard and bleak. He said, 'Your father and them others elected a lawman, girl. If they wanted a crook they shouldn't've voted for me.'

Whereupon he turned back into the jail office and, dropping heavily into a chair by the window, watched Susan Blake leave her horse at Joe Fagan's stable and then cross over to Elsie Adam's Millinery.

'It's comin',' he muttered, nervously pounding his right fist into the palm of his other hand. 'It's comin' sure as death. And that's what it'll be—death for a lot o' fellers fit to ride the river with!'

★　　★　　★

Red Valentine and Faro Savoy dismounted in front of the Senate Saloon, but Lee Beauregarde remained in saddle. 'Going to put up my hoss first,' he explained.

'Let the hide wait,' Valentine counselled, and pointed to Skillet brands on five slack-hipped horses at the hitchrack. 'If my friend Strebor is inside, we'll have free likker. Come on in and git wet.'

Savoy was already across the sidewalk. He said impatiently, 'To hell with the bronc-lovin' galoot. Let him do his drinkin' at the horse trough.'

'Mebbe that's where I'll do it,' Beauregarde muttered, and rode on down the street.

He passed Lorillard's Mercantile and was in front of the jail when Sheriff Derbyshire stepped out of the doorway and said, 'Just a minute, stranger.'

Beauregarde angled over to the sidewalk. 'What's on your mind?' he said.

The gaunt-faced lawman peered up at him in squint-eyed silence for a moment, as if

13

endeavoring to match what he saw with one of the reward dodgers on his desk. Then he said slowly, 'My name is Derbyshire and I'm the law in Panamint Valley. There's no rule ag'in killin' unbranded burros, but I don't cotton to fellers who use live targets for their funnin'.'

Beauregarde grinned. He said, 'You're warning the wrong gink, mister.'

'Mebbe not,' Derbyshire muttered. 'Mebbe you're still young enough to take a warnin'. You might do yourself a favor by ridin' right on through town, son—while you're still all in one piece.'

Something in the words, and in the way they were spoken, reminded Beauregarde of his dead father. This shaggy-browed sheriff with his big knuckled hands and saddle-warped legs was the same type of lawman Jeff Beauregarde had been. And Jeff had offered similar advice the day before he died; he'd ridden out to his son's rustler-ravaged horse ranch and said, 'You're bucking a bunch you can't beat, boy. Move out—while you're able to move.'

But there'd been a stubborn streak in Lee Beauregarde, and because of that streak, his father had died with a horse-thief's slug in his belly. Now another old man was giving him the same kind of advice.

'I might keep going at that,' Beauregarde said thoughtfully, 'after I take a look-see around.'

'You looking for anything special?' Derbyshire inquired.

A brittle glint came into Beauregarde's eyes, and he said very softly, 'Yeah—I'm looking for a dirty stinker named Roberts.'

'Don't reckon you'll find him here,' Derbyshire said. 'Nobody by that name ever lived in Panamint Valley.'

Beauregarde nudged back his flat Texas hat. A lock of black hair slid across his forehead, giving his trail-toughened face a youthful, almost boyish appearance. 'After three years of looking, I'm beginning to wonder if this Roberts lives anywhere,' he reflected, and rode on to Joe Fagan's livery.

Presently, when his leg-weary bronc had been cared for, Beauregarde stood in the stable doorway, giving Main Street a drifter's casual consideration. Apache Tank, he reflected, was like a dozen desert towns he'd ridden through. They were all pretty much alike, these back-country settlements. All built without definite plan or purpose, differing only in name and size and the number of saloons. This town had two—the Senate and the Silver Dollar—on the same side of the street, separated by the Elite Restaurant, Lorillard's Mercantile and the Wells Fargo stage office. Facing these false-fronted structures were the Acme Hotel, Elsie Adam's Millinery, the Panamint Valley Bank and the jail.

Little Joe Fagan came out of the barn, his wizened, gnomelike face made lopsided by the bulge of chewing tobacco in his cheek. 'Looks plum' peaceable, don't it?' he offered.

Beauregarde nodded.

'But it won't be peaceable long,' Fagan prophesied. 'We're agoin' to have high-wheeled hell in this country, stranger. We're agoin' to have a goddam war with all the fancy fixin's!'

'So?' Beauregarde prompted.

Fagan squinted at a green-bellied horse fly on the watering trough. He sucked in his dwarfish cheeks, puckered his lips and squirted an amber stream that plastered the fly dead center. Then he said, 'There'll be a meetin' of the Panamint Pool this evenin'. Some of the members is already in town, and so's the Skillet crew. Them two factions is slated for collision sooner or later, and today might be the day.'

'What's the trouble about?' Beauregarde inquired.

'Grass and water,' Fagan said. 'Just grass and water.'

He glanced at Beauregarde's tied-down holster then and asked, 'Say, you ain't one of the riders Strebor has been threatenin' to import, are you?'

Beauregarde grinned. This little liveryman had plenty of brass, inquiring into a man's private business. Ignoring the question,

16

Beauregarde said, 'Reckon I'll take on some vittles,' and walked leisurely toward the Elite Restaurant.

A blond, range-garbed man and a girl in a blue calico dress came down an outside stairway from the second floor of the Mercantile Building. Something in the considerate, cautious way the man escorted his companion caught Beauregarde's attention. They looked too young to be married, yet he glimpsed a gold band on the girl's left hand. Then he noticed the shingle which hung above the upstairs door—'Dr. J. B. Dulaine, M.D.'

Watching them come down the long stairway, and guessing the reason for the young husband's solicitous manner, Beauregarde felt a familiar sense of aloneness—a nagging, unnamed lack that had mocked him from many a back-trail campfire. There were times when a man felt the full penalty of the gunsmoke brand, when a drifter's role seemed entirely futile.

And because he had long ago placed a certain price on the end of his lone-wolf drifting, Beauregarde smiled a mirthless, self-mocking smile. The fine unity of those two people on the stairway wasn't for such as he; that young husband wasn't wearing a gun dedicated to revenge . . .

Beauregarde shrugged, and was about to cross the Elite stoop when he saw a gun-hung rider step out of the Mercantile doorway and collide with the couple on the sidewalk.

The husband snapped, 'Watch where you're going, Casco!' and pushed the rider back on his heels.

Casco snarled, 'Watch your own self, Ellison!'

And in that instant Lee Beauregarde remembered what little Joe Fagan had told him—'*them two factions is slated for collision!*'

He saw the girl grasp her husband's arm, heard her say excitedly, 'Oscar—don't fuss with him! Please don't!'

Ellison obediently escorted his wife across the board walk and helped her into the ranch rig at the curb. His fair-skinned face was flushed; he looked like a kid suddenly confronted with the necessity of being a man—of accepting a man's responsibility—and not knowing just how to handle this chore. He was on the point of climbing into the wagon when Casco called tauntingly, 'Still yeller as the hair on your head, ain't you, Oscar!'

Ellison turned and said quickly, 'I'm taking my wife to the hotel. Then I'll come looking for you.'

'I won't be hard to find,' Casco promised, and licked his thick lips. 'I'll be waiting for you in front of the Senate.'

Ellison climbed into the rig. As he swung the team in a wide turn, his wife

18

exclaimed hysterically, 'You mustn't, Oscar! You mustn't. He'll kill you, honey—He'll kill you sure!'

Beauregarde was thinking about that as he stood watching Casco saunter along the street, low-slung gun swaying gently to his swaggering stride. *She's right*, he thought: *Ellison won't have a chance . . .*

Instead of going into the restaurant, Beauregarde went back to the livery where Joe Fagan stood in the doorway.

'That's the start of it,' the liveryman announced. 'Today's the day, just like I said!'

'Who's Casco?' Beauregarde asked.

'Foreman of the Skillet. That's his boss talkin' to him now over there on the Senate stoop. Sid Strebor—who's fixin' to be a reg'lar goddam cattle king.'

Beauregarde glanced that way, and saw a dark-faced man with a spiked black mustache standing between Valentine and Savoy. Strebor was a head shorter than the two trail tramps, yet even at that distance Beauregarde sensed a sharpness and an arrogance in Strebor that compensated for his lack of stature.

'Ellison belong to the Pool?' Beauregarde inquired, half resenting the interest he felt for the yellow-haired young husband.

'Yeah, but that ain't the main trouble between 'em. Casco was sweet on Della

19

before she married Oscar. He thought he was the main hombre around this country and he ain't got over the idee yet. Oscar won out, but he won't win this time, not with guns. He'll be coroner meat—and him married to as fine a filly as ever wore a bustle!'

'Seem like nice folks, the Ellisons,' Beauregarde reflected.

'They be. They got a little place up in the Dragoon Hills—the O Bar E. Looks like it'll be the first widow-woman brand in Panamint Valley.'

Then, as if suddenly remembering the question Beauregarde had ignored a few minutes before, Fagan asked, 'Say—didn't you come here to ride for the Skillet?'

'Yes,' Beauregarde admitted, and seeing quick caution clamp Fagan's features, smiled a little inside. This gabby liveryman was thinking he'd talked too much; Fagan was figuring he'd given information to an imported gunhawk . . .

'Then if you're a Skillet man what you doin' hangin' around here?' Fagan demanded resentfully. 'Why don't you go over there with the rest of that riffraff bunch?'

'I am,' Beauregarde said. 'I'm going over there right now.'

★   ★   ★

Susan Blake was leaving Elsie Adams' Millinery when Casco flung his insulting accusation at Ellison. She heard young Oscar's anger-prodded threat, and saw the stark fear in Della Ellison's eyes as the wagon rolled toward the Acme hotel. Whereupon she hurried along the walk, and joined the couple as they went up the veranda steps.

Della's doll-like face was white as the cameo brooch at her throat. 'Oh, Susan—he's going to fight Casco!' she exclaimed. 'He won't listen to me at all!'

'Now, now,' Susan said, and nodded toward the veranda bench. 'You're in no condition to get upset, honey. Let's talk this over.'

She and Della sat down, but the pressure of impending conflict was too strong in Oscar to allow him to relax. He said, 'This is something that talk can't change. Buck Casco has been spoiling for a fight ever since I married Della, and talking won't change him. I've took my last insult.'

Susan forced a smile and said soothingly, 'I don't blame you, Oscar. I don't blame you at all. He's got too big for his britches since Strebor made him foreman. But this isn't the time to fight him, not with Della like she is. It might mark the baby.'

'There's worse things than being marked by a gun fight,' Ellison said doggedly. 'Being branded the son of a yellow-haired coward is

21

one of them. I wouldn't want a son to grow up with that kind of a mark on him.'

Susan smiled again, and asked, 'What makes you so sure it'll be a boy?'

But that subterfuge didn't interrupt the single line of Ellison's thinking. He kept glancing at the Senate, as if beckoned by a beacon he couldn't resist. He pulled out his makings, fumbled for a paper, then put the Durham sack back without opening it. Susan knew then that he was scared . . . He didn't trust his fingers enough to shape up a cigarette!

And knowing that, she understood how little chance he'd have against a confident, coldblooded gunslinger like Buck Casco. Yet because she had lived all her life with a father who put pride above everything else, she understood that nothing she could say would divert Ellison from dying for his pride over there in the dust. All men—even very young men—had some sort of code that bound them. It might be futile, senseless code whereby they sacrificed their lives for something they called principle, pride of self-respect; but their stolid acceptance of it never wavered once they possessed it.

Della, too, seemed to sense the futility of further pleading. She sat slumped like a woman grown suddenly old, her large brown eyes gone grim and lusterless. She said haltingly, 'I'll pray for you, Oscar, but God doesn't look kindly on gunfighters. The Bible says to turn the other cheek.'

'I've done that,' Ellison insisted, a plain note of tension in his voice. 'I've turned both cheeks already, time and again. But this time I can't, Della. I can't!'

He bent over and kissed her on the forehead and was turning to leave when Susan exclaimed, 'Look—look over there!'

★   ★   ★

Leaving the livery, Lee Beauregarde walked toward the Senate Saloon without hurry and without hesitation. It was mid-afternoon now and the sun was behind him, its strong rays sending a constant heat on his high shoulders. And because the turbulent years had schooled Beauregarde into a habitual regard for small details, a secretive smile came to his lips. This play would be against every tenet of a gunslinger's creed; it would be as near to deliberate foolishness as he'd ever come. But he would have one thing in his favor—*the slanting rays of the sun!*

A wagon came down Main Street with a man and a woman on the seat and three half-grown kids dangling their bare feet from the tailboard. When the rig turned into the Mercantile wagonyard, a paunchy, aproned old man on the store stoop called, 'Howdy, Jeb—howdy, Miz Hodnett.'

There was the cordiality of real friendship in their greetings, which was another lack Lee Beauregarde had long felt. It had been three years since anyone had greeted him in so friendly a fashion—three years of futile, lone-wolf wandering. When he walked past the store the aproned merchant looked at him with judging eyes and then glanced across the street to where Sheriff Derbyshire stood in the jail doorway. It was a trivial thing, that glance; but the inference was plain to Beauregarde. Gus Lorillard was using this method of telling a gunhung stranger that there was a lawman in town.

Casco still stood on the saloon stoop with Strebor, Red Valentine and Savoy. There were three other men there now who Beauregarde guessed were Skillet riders. And all those yonderly eyes were squinted against the sun's harsh glare. When he shifted his glance to the Acme Hotel he saw the Ellison couple on the veranda with the blonde-haired girl he'd met out on the flats. Recalling how she'd said, 'Your kind of *killer*,' Beauregarde smiled again. She would soon be seeing how his kind of killer handled a gun.

He was thinking about that when Red Valentine called, 'Takes you a damn long time to stable a hoss. Come on up and meet some friends of mine.'

Beauregarde didn't answer. He was within fifteen feet of the stoop now, which was as close as he cared to be. Ignoring Valentine and the others, he stared deliberately at Buck Casco, and said, 'I hear you're looking for trouble.'

Casco's eyes bulged wide with astonishment. He held his left hand in an eye-shading gesture, peered below it and demanded, 'Who in hell are you?'

His voice carried a plain puzzlement, and because Beauregarde knew what curiosity could do to a man, he quickly followed up this advantage. 'I'm the galoot who dislikes widow makers,' he said.

Red Valentine came part way across the stoop. He took off his hat and scratched his roan-thatched head and peered at Beauregarde. 'You gone *loco?*' he demanded. 'this is Strebor's foreman you're talkin' to, Texican!'

Beauregarde sent a roving glance at the hotel veranda, saw Ellison kiss his wife—and knew how little time remained. This thing had to be speeded up; it had to be rushed to a quick climax. 'Casco doesn't look like a foreman to me,' he drawled.

Then his voice turned thin and sharp and insolent. 'Casco doesn't look like a man at all. He looks like a polecat—and he stinks like a polecat!'

25

The effect of that declaration was instantaneous. Red Valentine halted in midstride. The men on the stoop stiffened; they stepped back against the saloon wall as if motivated by a ritual long rehearsed. Buck Casco went into a gunman's crabwise crouch; the fingers of his right hand splayed into clutching claws above his holstered gun.

Yet even then, even with killer courage flaming hot and bright in his slitted eyes, Casco's curiosity held him captive for a moment longer. 'Why you mixin' into this deal?' he demanded.

'For a reason you wouldn't understand,' Beauregarde drawled, and deliberately switched his gaze to Sid Strebor, who stood watching all this with a gambler's inexpressive mask on his hawk-featured face.

It was an old trick, that switch; a trick worn thin by long usage. But it worked. It made Buck Casco think he had a chance for a sneak draw—lured him into the belief that he was bucking a careless, overconfident man. His clawing fingers darted down and snatched his gun from its holster. He was standing like that, with the weapon half raised, when Beauregarde fired.

No man there on Main Street had seen Beauregarde draw. It was so incredibly fast and smooth that their eyes couldn't catch it. But they saw Casco stagger back as if hit by

26

an invisible hammer—saw his gun slip from fingers that clutched spasmodically at a hole in his shirt pocket.

The Skillet foreman slumped back against the saloon wall, squirming a little, like a man with an itching back. His hot eyes continued to stare at Beauregarde. His slack-jawed mouth sagged open and his knees buckled slowly, like rust-weakened hinges—until finally he fell face down and lay motionless as a bundle of discarded old clothes.

For a tautly suspended interval no one moved and no one spoke. The pungent aroma of Con Dooly's blacksmith forge drifted in from the alley, and down at Fagan's livery a horse stomped restlessly. The moments crawled on, carrying their cargo of hushed expectancy. The silence got tighter and tighter; it pulled Beauregarde's nerves into thin strands of rash eagerness. His gun was holstered; his right hand hung free, and he was waiting for the play he felt sure would come—the wolf-pack play which the smell of blood always brought.

Sid Strebor stepped over to Casco's body. He reached down and pressed a small, brown-fingered hand against his foreman's bloody shirt. Then he said, 'Deader than last year's beef drive.'

There was neither anger nor regret in Strebor's voice, just a flat statement of fact.

27

He stood up and wiped his hand on the seat of his pants and peered at Beauregarde with no visible sign of emotion in his piercing black eyes.

'You work fast,' he said. 'Too goddam fast.'

'Want to make something out of it?' Beauregarde asked quietly.

Strebor shook his head. 'Not just now,' he said thoughtfully. 'Not just now.'

Those three repeated words told Beauregarde all he needed to know about Sid Strebor. Or so he thought. His mind catalogued Skillet's boss swiftly and exactly, tagging Strebor as a man without pride—as a member of that cold-blooded, calculating breed which bides its time the same way a crooked gambler awaits a gimmick game.

Sheriff Derbyshire stepped up beside Beauregarde. He said bluntly, 'We've had enough shooting for one day. You'd best be drifting.'

'Suits me,' Beauregarde agreed, already feeling the nausea that invariably gripped him after a shootout.

He was turning away when Sid Strebor demanded harshly, 'Aren't you arresting him, Derbyshire?'

'What for?' the sheriff asked.

'What for?' Strebor snapped, and pointed toward Casco's sprawled body. 'He just killed my foreman in cold blood, didn't he? What better reason would you want for arresting a man?'

Derbyshire hooked his thumbs into the armholes of his vest and surveyed Strebor with unruffled calm. If the old lawman bore Skillet's owner any ill will, it didn't show in his face, nor in his voice when he said, 'I couldn't see the start of it. But from where I stood it looked like an even break all around.'

Which was when Gus Lorillard and Jeb Hodnett strode up.

'I saw the whole play,' the merchant announced, and glanced wonderingly at Lee Beauregarde. 'The stranger gave Buck all the best of it Sam. Casco grabbed first.'

And Hodnett said, 'He sure did. It was the darn'est thing ever I see. Looked like Buck had him caught flat-footed. The stranger wasn't even watchin' him—but he got his gun out faster'n water slidin' off goose grease. By God, he's *fast*!'

The big-boned fingers of Derbyshire's left hand absently tapped the silver star on his vest pocket. He said, 'Thanks for the information, boys. Then he looked at Strebor, saying civilly, 'I'm taking the word of disinterested witnesses, Sid. You heard what they said. It's no skin off their nose, one way or the other. They're telling it like it was.'

Strebor's dark face showed no sign of anger. But there was a cutting rasp to his voice when he said, 'So that's the way it's to be—every man for himself and to hell with law and order. That suits me, Derbyshire. By God, it suits me fine. From now on the Skillet will shoot first, and talk about it afterward!'

'I've never took sides,' Derbyshire said patiently. 'I'm taking none now. But I'm warning you to be careful with your shooting.'

'We will. We will,' Strebor promised, a confident, almost pleased note coming into his voice. 'From here out we'll be careful that we don't waste any slugs.'

He turned to his riders, said, 'Couple of you boys carry Casco over to the undertaker's,' and then went back into the saloon.

Derbyshire moved close to Beauregarde. 'You killed one man today and you saved another man,' he said very softly. 'I don't know why you made a play like that, son—but I'm pleasured that you did.'

Then he strode over to the group which had gathered in front of Lorillard's Mercantile.

From long habit Beauregarde took out his gun and rejected the spent shell. He was replacing it with a fresh one when Red Valentine came over to him.

'What in hell hit you?' he demanded. 'what made you mix it up with Casco?'

There was a wary expression in Valentine's eyes—a new note of respect in his voice. It was, Beauregarde knew, the grudging admiration

30

of one killer for another. And because nausea's sickening grip was having its way with him, Beauregarde sensed the full irony of Valentine's admiration. The red-haired renegade didn't know what it was to get sick every time he killed a man. Valentine gloried in his gun skill—took pride in his knack for swift slaughter. But Lee Beauregarde wasn't geared that way.

'Why did you cut Casco down?' Valentine insisted.

'Mebbe I didn't like the way he wore his face,' Beauregarde said gruffly, and slid his gun into its holster.

Valentine's tawny eyes showed a fuller puzzlement. 'Well, I'll be a sway-backed son of a sheep-herder's slut!' he blurted. 'You wouldn't shoot a burro, but you kill a man on account of you don't like his looks!'

Then he said slyly, 'Say—I might still be able to talk Sid into hirin' you, if you'll quit usin' Skillet riders for targets. There's goin' to be plenty fun in this country from here on, and Sid pays good wages.'

'Not interested,' Beauregarde muttered.

He crossed the street and, going leisurely along the plank walk, saw Oscar Ellison standing on the hotel steps with an arm around his young wife. The blonde girl was with them, her lips gently smiling. When he was about to pass, she said, 'Mister Beauregarde.'

He halted and lifted his hat, and she said, 'These folks want to thank you for—for what you did over there. Oscar and Della Ellison.'

The smile lingered on her lips, but there was an ill-concealed reserve in her voice, and in the speculative gaze of her blue eyes.

'Your fight with Casco was a big favor to me,' Ellison declared. 'It saved me from having to meet him. I might not've been lucky as you were.'

His boyish face also wore a smile. His voice was entirely pleasant; yet there was that same note of reserve that Beauregarde had recognized in the blonde girl's voice. This yellow-haired rider, Beauregarde guessed, looked upon him as a ruthless gunsmoke pariah—as a man apart from other men. Soundless, cynical laughter ran through Beauregarde, and merged with the gnawing sickness inside him—the sickness he felt every time he killed a man.

'I had my reasons for killing Casco,' he said briefly.

Whereupon Della Ellison did a strange thing. At least it seemed strange to Beauregarde. She held out her hand and smiled at him without any reserve at all. 'I saw you standing in front of the restaurant while Oscar was arguing with Casco,' she said.

Beauregarde took her hand, felt its firm pressure and was strongly aware of the warm gratitude in her upturned eyes. She nodded at her husband and the blonde girl, saying, 'They insist that you didn't do it on our account. But I choose to believe you did, and I thank you from the bottom of my heart.'

The gratitude in her voice and in her eyes was like a soothing lotion. But it couldn't cure the clutching sickness at the pit of Beauregarde's stomach. There was only one cure for that—a bottle and a glass and the quilted numbness whiskey brought to a man who seldom drank it.

Releasing Mrs. Ellison's hand, he bowed with an almost forgotten gallantry, said, 'Thank you, ma'am,' and walked hurriedly toward the Silver Dollar Saloon.

CHAPTER TWO

Buck Casco's killing was the chief topic of conversation in Apache Tank for hours. Tongues wagged in every doorway on Main Street and along the alleys that crossed it. Men who'd seen the fight described it to those who hadn't; but no man could offer a reasonable explanation of why the tall stranger had chosen to end the Ellison-Casco feud in such dramatic and unexpected fashion . . .

'Must of been bad blood between them two

at some time in the past,' Jeb Hodnett decided, sitting on a sorghum keg at Lorillard's store. 'This Beauregarde was no friend of Ellison. Oscar says he never seen him before in his life.'

Cliff Paddock came in through the alley door, his clothes carrying the pungent odor of Con Dooly's blacksmith shop. Medium tall and compactly built, he had the broad shoulders and slim hips of a riding man. 'That sorrel stud is the devil's own image to shoe,' he remarked, and ordered a cigar.

Then he asked, 'You boys got the long-legged smokeroo figgered out yet?'

'No,' Gus Lorillard admitted. 'We ain't. There's no rhyme nor reason to what he did. He wasn't drunk and he hadn't even spoke to Casco, as far as anybody knows. It's downright mysterious, for a fact.'

Paddock said, 'Perhaps Buck could tell us, if he could talk.'

Which was the consensus of opinion in Apache Tank...

Down at the stable, Joe Fagan was delivering a full report of the affair to Dave Blake, who had just driven in from his Three Links ranch. 'Somethin' damn peculiar about this galoot Beauregarde,' Joe concluded. 'He tells me he came here to ride for the Skillet. Then he walks over to the Senate and cuts Casco down like he's stompin' a fly on a dung heap.'

34

Blake tugged thoughtfully at his down-swirling mustache. A slow smile creased his craggy, age-wrinkled face, and he said finally, 'Beauregarde might be just what the medico ordered—a first class gunslinger.'

Fagan blinked. 'You mean *you* sent for him?' he demanded.

'No, I didn't send for him. But, by grab, I'm going to hire him, if he'll wait a spell for his wages.'

Paddock strolled over from the Mercantile and saluted Fagan and Blake in friendly fashion. 'What do you think of the shooting, Dave?' he inquired.

'I think this Beauregarde is going to move into my empty bunkhouse, providing I can talk him into a deal,' Blake announced.

This declaration didn't seem to surprise Paddock, nor particularly impress him. He leaned indolently against the door frame and built a cigarette. Standing there with hat pushed back on his curly brown hair and a good-natured grin on his face, he was almost handsome.

'Professional gunhawks come high,' he reflected, tapering the cigarette and licking it. 'Especially high class killers like this Beauregarde seems to be.'

'He'd be worth what he costs,' Blake said grimly. 'If every outfit in the Pool had hired a gunhawk riding for it, Strebor wouldn't be crowding this range like he is. There's a big difference between deviling a bunch of family men—and stacking up against gunslick galoots who got nothing to lose but their hides.'

Paddock nodded agreement. He glanced along the street and said casually, 'They say Beauregarde is drinking himself into a one-man spree at the Silver Dollar.'

'Mebbeso he's celebratin' the new notch on his gun,' Joe Fagan suggested, and puckered his lips preparatory to showering a fly . . .

Up the street, at the Senate bar, Red Valentine endeavored to explain Beauregarde's queer behavior to Sid Strebor. 'Can't figger it out,' Valentine admitted. 'Lee didn't come here to side the Pool. I'm certain of that. He was with us over in New Mexico, ridin' for Alex McSween. And he had a gun rep in Texas before that.'

'He's got a gun rep here now,' Strebor muttered. 'Casco was supposed to be fast. But your Lincoln County chum made him look slower than sorghum with the frost bite.'

Faro Savoy gulped down his fifth drink. 'To hell with Casco and Beauregarde both,' he wheezed. 'Casco is dead, and Beauregarde soon will be. I'll chop down that proud-faced bastard and spit in his goddam eye!'

Strebor ignored the reedy rider's bragging. He motioned for Valentine to move closer. 'Like I wrote,' he said softly, 'there's a fortune

36

to be made in this valley—and I intend to make it. There's grass and water enough for one damned big cow spread, which is what Skillet is slated to be. Starting right now you're drawing foreman's pay, plus a slice in the profits later on.'

'That's fine,' Valentine said. 'You've done hired a foreman.'

'Don't go sticking your snout out like Casco did,' Strebor muttered. 'A real smart man don't need to be fast with a gun. Buck didn't die on account of his speed with guns, but because he wanted to run after every damn female that struck his fancy. If he'd tended to business instead of chasing skirts, he'd have made enough money with me to buy a barnful of women in a couple of years.'

'Yeah,' said Valentine. 'A gink don't have to worry about wimmin if he's got plenty *dinero*. What we figger to win here, Sid?'

Strebor made an open-palmed gesture with a hand small and soft as a woman's hand. 'The whole shebang,' he said. 'Panamint Valley, lock, stock and barel.'

A low whistle hissed between Valentine's teeth and a greedy glint came into his eyes. 'You're cookin' with coal oil,' he said gustily. 'You sure as hell are!'

Then he asked, 'How about this Pool? They got a good organization?'

'Fair,' Strebor admitted. 'Dave Blake is

37

running it, and he's nobody's fool. His Three Links was a big outfit until the drought whittled it down a couple years back. Now he's just hanging on by his boot straps, but he won't sell. He's lined up every outfit in the valley to buck me, but they're all two-bit brands, Red. And I've got an ace in the hole—an ace the Pool can't beat.'

'What kind of an ace?' Valentine asked, plainly curious.

But Sid Strebor shook his head and said secretively, 'I said an ace in the hole. Which is the proper place for it to be.'

★　　★　　★

At sundown Lee Beauregarde sat alone at a table in the Silver Dollar Saloon. The bottle of bourbon in front of him was well down toward the halfway mark, but Beauregarde wasn't drunk. He sat slack muscled, hat brim tilted to protect him against the light cast by a high chandelier above the bar, idly watching Honest John Ogden serve his Saturday night customers.

It was characteristic of Beauregarde that even here, while he was endeavoring to drug the reaction of a killing, he sat with a wall behind him—the bar and the batwing gates at right angles in front of him. The turbulent years had brought him a full measure of caution; they had taught him that the price of survival was more than mere speed with a gun—it was a vigilance so constant that wariness became an integral part of a man's mind.

Recalling the many times he'd sat like this, waiting and watching, hoping for some sign or word that would give him a clue to his father's killer, Beauregarde frowned. A man could spend the best years of his life in futile searching; he could grow old and crusty without winning the reward he sought. The object of his vengeance might no longer exist. Roberts might be dead, or he might be locked up in some prison. If that were so, he would never find Roberts, and it was this possibility which filled Beauregarde with slogging futility as he sat there, not quite drunk and not quite sober . . .

He watched six range-garbed men tromp in from the street, moving as a group and lining up at the bar in the fashion of old acquaintances. Tallying those faces in the back-bar mirror, Beauregarde recognized Oscar Ellison and Jeb Hodnett. It occurred to him then that these men were members of the Panamint Pool, probably just finished with their meeting. He was thinking about that, and wondering what chance the Pool would have against the Skillet's gunhawk outfit, when he saw Ellison accompany a saddle-warped oldster across the room.

They came directly to Beauregarde's table, and Ellison said, 'Mister Beauregarde, meet Dave Blake. He's president of the Pool.'

Beauregarde nodded, not getting up nor offering his hand. He said, 'Howdy,' and motioned to a chair. 'Have a drink.'

Blake sat down, and as Ellison turned back to the bar, said, 'They tell me you're some fast with a gun—that you gave Casco the jump and then beat him easy.'

Beauregarde waggled a finger at Honest John. He called, 'Bring another glass, please, sir,' and then asked bluntly, 'What's on your mind, Blake?'

'Considerable,' Blake admitted. 'Anyone told you what we're up against here?'

Honest John set a glass on the table. Whereupon Beauregarde poured a drink, pushed it across to Blake and watched him drink it. Studying this man's aquiline, aristocratic face, Beauregarde had an impelling feeling that he'd seen Blake somewhere; that he should recognize him by another name. But Joe Fagan had told him Blake's Three Links outfit was the oldest brand in the valley—that Blake had lived there for thirty years.

He said finally, 'Yes, I hear there's going to be trouble. But what's that got to do with me?'

Blake wiped his drooping mustache with

the back of an age-blotched hand. He peered at Beauregarde in a speculative, deliberately judging way, and said, 'That depends on a couple of things.'

'Such as what?'

'Well, on why you killed Buck Casco; for instance.'

Beauregarde's lamplit face showed a faint amusement. A lot of people were wondering about that same thing, he guessed. Yet even if he told them the reason they wouldn't believe it. They wouldn't swallow the proposition that a six-gun smokeroo had killed a man he'd never seen before just to save another man whom he'd never spoken to until after the fight. Fiddle-footed saddle tramps didn't do things like that, unless they were drunk. And he'd been as sober as a circuit gospel singer.

'Mind telling why you did it?' Blake inquired.

'What difference would it make?'

Blake's sharp old eyes kept studying him; kept searching. 'Well, Mrs. Ellison seems to think you did it to save young Oscar from getting his pants shot off. If that's correct, then you'll be interested in my offer.'

So that was it! This keen-eyed old cowman was guessing there might be a soft streak in him. Blake was wise enough to know that any man might do a foolish, hasty thing—even a six-gun smokeroo. And Blake wanted to annex

41

his gun help on a more honorable basis than the offer of fighting wages!

'My reason was a private one,' Beauregarde muttered. 'I'm not interested in your argument with Strebor. Come sun-up I'm pulling my picket pin.'

Blake's eyes narrowed, and he said, 'So you weren't saving young Ellison when you jumped Casco!'

Beauregarde ignored the question. He poured another round of drinks, and seeing color stain Blake's cheeks, felt sure he'd seen this man's face some other time. He was wondering about that, vainly striving to bring the remote memory into sharper focus, when Blake's eyes blinked wide and the cowman pushed the table over in a way that knocked Beauregarde back against the wall.

In that same instant a gun exploded. But even before the blast filled the salon with room-trapped sound, Beauregarde heard the wicked swish of a slug that missed his head by inches. All this in the time it took him to scramble up from his chair; to swivel around and see a reedy shape slink away from the saloon's rear door . . .

Honest John yelled, 'Who was that?'

And Dave Blake exclaimed, 'Some stranger taking a sneak shot at Beauregarde!'

Three of the men ran to the rear door. They peered into the alley's quilted gloom, and one of them called, 'I hear him. He's running through the blacksmith yard!'

But Beauregarde paid no attention to the report. The glimpse he'd caught of the shape in the doorway had been enough to give him the skulker's identity. Faro Savoy had never liked him; the tubercular gunman was feeling his whiskey—wanting to score a quick killing for his new boss.

Glancing at the overturned bottle of bourbon, Beauregarde saw the last of its liquid run out on the littered floor. It was, he reflected, a sort of symbol; that spilled whiskey was like his luck. One day it too would run out . . .

He glanced at Blake, who stood silently regarding him. 'Thanks for saving my bacon,' he drawled. 'You tipped over the table just in time.'

Then, because Savoy's sneaking attack had placed him solidly in the man's debt, Beauregarde asked, 'What was the proposition you wanted to offer me?'

'I was going to ask you to take a job for gun wages, payable when the Pool ships beef next fall. We need a rider with gunslick savvy—a rider who can play the Skillet at its own game. You'd live at my place, but your job would be to keep an eye on Pool range and give a hand where needed.'

'How about Sheriff Derbyshire?'

43

Beauregarde inquired. 'Can't he send a deputy out to ride patrol?'

Blake's face showed a quick irritation. 'Derbyshire won't mix into it,' he explained. 'Sam has some stubborn ideas about his badge. Those ideas may cost him the next election.'

Then he asked, 'How about it? You interested in my proposition?'

Beauregarde smiled cynically. Fate had a way of messing up a man's plans. He had come here to ride for the Skillet with the idea that he might meet up with the murderer of his father. Then some deep-rooted strand of sympathy had prodded him into a Good Samaritan play to save Oscar Ellison, and afterward he'd decided to drift out of this country. Now, because Dave Blake had saved him from an assassin's slug, he had to side the Panamint Pool . . .

'Yeah,' he said. 'I'll take the job.'

Quick satisfaction came into Dave Blake's eyes. He said, 'Good—by God, I'm glad to hear that! Come on over and meet the men you'll be working for.' And he escorted Beauregarde to the bar.

'We've got us a gunrider,' Blake announced, then introduced Beauregarde to the four men who stood there with Oscar Ellison.

Jeb Hodnett gripped his hand with open admiration, and said, 'It done my gizzard good to see you outshoot that horrawin' son Casco!'

Tate Corvette, a skinny little man whom Blake introduced as having a wife, four youngsters and a twenty-year-old son, was meekly deferential. 'Glad to have you with us,' he declared. But he didn't look glad . . .

The third oldster—bulky, shiftless Hank Lundermann—was a widower with two sons who had 'high-tailed it for the tules' and a grown daughter named Judy. The Lazy L owner seemed to be feeling his liquor, for he clapped Beauregarde on the shoulder with a hand as big as a ham and bellowed for a new round of drinks.

'This is Cliff Paddock,' Blake said, poking a finger at the Boxed P owner. 'He's conniving around to be my son-in-law.'

Paddock grinned and shook hands. He had the easy-going manner of a good mixer, yet Beauregarde tallied him at once as being the most militant member of this crowd. There was a controlled hardness in his eyes, and in the vise-like grip of his fingers . . .

Presently, when Beauregarde had promised to report at Three Links in the morning, he went to the Elite and ordered a steak supper. Eating in leisurely fashion, he reviewed the day's fast-forming developments and felt a familiar sense of frustration. His plans seldom went according to schedule; they kept changing with the scenery—with each new twist in the trail. The pattern of his life was completely

45

unpredictable; it varied with every shift of the wind.

Remembering the blonde-haired girl who had introduced him to the Ellisons, he wondered if she was Hank Lundermann's daughter. There was no family resemblance. The Lazy L owner had a rough, scrubstock appearance, whereas the blonde girl had a look of good breeding. And she was the most beautiful girl he'd ever seen. Of that he was convinced . . .

Finished with his meal, Beauregarde strolled out to the street and shaped up a smoke. Rigs and riders were leaving town, and their concentrated departure raised a high screen of dust along Main Street. Hank Lundermann tooled a crooked-wheeled wagon away from the hotel and, as he passed that way, called, '*Buenos noches, amigo.*'

There was a dark-haired girl on the seat with him. Beauregarde caught a brief glimpse of her red-lipped smile as the wagon went on, and because he was hugely relieved to know that Hank's daughter wasn't blonde, Beauregarde smiled also. He knew then how completely one girl's fine blue eyes had captured his interest, and more—his unqualified admiration. When he lit his cigarette his face showed a perplexed frown in the match flare . . .

Sheriff Derbyshire quartered over from the jail and said, 'I couldn't find no trace of that galoot in the alley. You got any ideas who it was shot at you?'

Beauregarde broke the match stick and flicked it out into the dust. 'No,' he lied, not choosing to discuss his personal affairs with the worried old lawman. 'Probably some drunk wanting a new notch on his gun.'

Derbyshire eyed him with squinting puzzlement. 'I had a hunch you'd know who it was, and I still got the same hunch. Leastwise I'm figgerin' it was one of the Skillet's men.' Then he added, 'Hear you've signed on with Blake.'

Beauregarde nodded, whereupon Sheriff Derbyshire's voice took on a plain note of resignation. 'You put a lot of puzzles into a man's mind, son. You do for a fact.'

He went back across the street then, and Beauregarde headed for the livery stable. He was approaching Lorillard's Mercantile when Jeb Hodnett drove his team out of the wagonyard. Beauregarde halted and stood waiting for the rig to cross the sidewalk. Hodnett glanced down and, recognizing him in the store's reflected light, nodded a wordless greeting, Mrs. Hodnett's face held a tight-lipped coldness and she took no notice of him beyond one brief, searching glance. But the three boys sitting on a crate at the rear of the wagon all stared at him with open admiration, and the oldest called: 'Howdy, gunslinger!'

Beauregarde grinned and went on. Dave Blake came out of the Mercantile toting a sack of flour. The Pool boss boosted his burden into a wagon at the curb beside which Cliff Paddock stood with the blonde girl. These two were holding the reins of saddled horses; and they made a singularly well-matched couple standing there together. For a reason he couldn't define, Lee Beauregarde resented that picture.

When he came on, Dave Blake said, 'Meet my daughter Susan, Beauregarde.'

That surprised Beauregarde completely. He'd guessed, of course, that she was the daughter of a cowman; that much had been plain to him from the moment he'd first seen her. But it hadn't occurred to him that she was Dave Blake's daughter.

She turned toward him, this move bringing her face into the shadows; making it an indistinct oval against the yonderly lamplight. She said, 'We've already met, Dad.' Then she added, 'I hear you're going to move into our empty bunkhouse, Mister Beauregarde.'

Her voice was civil, nothing more. It was the exact tone a proud girl might use in talking to a hired hand of no particular importance—a hired hand for whom she felt slight regard.

Beauregarde said, 'Yes,' and was strongly aware of Cliff Paddock's continuing appraisal.

'Better come on along with us now,' Blake

48

suggested, climbing into the wagon. 'Then you'll be all set to take a look-see around first thing in the morning. There's no telling how soon trouble will start.'

Beauregarde was on the verge of refusing this invitation when Susan said, 'Why don't you? Cliff rides only part way with us. We'd be glad to have your company.'

Whereupon Beauregarde nodded, and said, 'I'll go get my hoss.'

★   ★   ★

Leaving Apache Tank, Susan rode between Beauregarde and Paddock, far enough behind the wagon to escape the wheel-churned dust. As they went across the flats at a brisk canter, she couldn't distinguish these men's faces; but later, when a three-quarter moon topped the valley's east wall and they climbed the Dragoon Hills at a slower pace, Susan covertly studied Lee Beauregarde's moonlit features.

It was, she decided, a strong face. And good-looking, in a rough-and-tumble sort of way. The brittle hardness of his eyes didn't show in the soft light; the v-shaped scar on his cheek was like a long dimple now, and he looked ten years younger. Recalling the wistful, almost hungry expression she'd glimpsed in his eyes that afternoon, she wondered about him; and wondered why

49

she should feel so strong an interest in him.

Surely this man's gunsmoke brand was plain to read. Even though she sensed complexities in his nature that were at variance with his brand, Lee Beauregarde was a gunhawk. He'd proved that by admitting to Joe Fagan that he had come there to ride for the Skillet. The unexplained fight with Buck Casco had spoiled his plans, but it had proved how skilled Beauregarde was in the art of swift slaughter. Only a professional gunman could have given such an amazing exhibition of nerveless speed and precision . . .

Deliberately then, Susan compared these two men riding silently beside her. Cliff Paddock, who had settled in Panamint Valley a year before, seemed as open and easy to understand as Beauregarde was difficult. Cliff, she reflected, was a good-natured, industrious young cowman who'd made himself well liked in the valley. Beauregarde, on the other hand, was a drifter; a man of dark moods and taciturn ways. He seemed always on guard, never showing more of his inner self than he wanted others to see.

The difference between them showed in their talk now as Paddock asked, 'What's your idea on the Pool's chances of beating the Skillet, Beauregarde?'

'Can't give an opinion,' the tall Texan

drawled. 'Don't know enough about the two outfits.'

'Unless Strebor brings in more riders, we're about even in numbers,' Susan explained.

Beauregarde considered that information for a moment. Then he said thoughtfully, 'Well, range wars are bad. No matter who wins, everybody loses.'

Paddock chuckled. 'That sounds right strange, coming from you,' he declared. 'I thought all Texicans were natural born battlers.'

'Mebbeso,' Beauregarde muttered, taking note of the slightly jeering note in Paddock's voice, and wondering at it. 'But that doesn't change the grief a range war brings to a country. I saw it in New Mexico, and it's not a nice thing to see.'

The talk died down then, and little more was said until they reached the Boxed P turn-off at the top of Gooseneck Divide. Here Dave Blake halted the wagon and called, 'Keep your eyes peeled and your powder dry, Cliff.'

Paddock chuckled again and, reaching out, gave Susan a brief, one-armed embrace. He said, '*Hasta luego*, folks,' and put his horse to a hard run.

For a time then, while they crossed the divide, Beauregarde probed his mind for some clue that would aid him in tallying Cliff Paddock. It was a long established custom,

51

this habit of placing an exact judgment upon every man he met. At first he had done it deliberately, knowing that all men couldn't be classified as good or bad—dangerous or harmless. There were fine shadings of difference in each classification, and the knowledge of these deviations had more than once tipped the balance in an even-up fight.

But Beauregarde hadn't yet catalogued Paddock to his satisfaction when they reached the divide's rim and Susan said, 'There's Three Links, off to the west.'

Beauregarde gazed out across this secondary valley and glimpsed a moon-silvered windmill above a rambling house. Three Links huddled against the triple-toed base of a long, low mesa, its 'dobe-walled house and sprawling corrals showing plainly against the brush-blotched slants beyond. It was, he saw at once, a large and well arranged lay-out. The house had a full length gallery which faced the valley. Beyond the main house was a long building which he guessed to be the bunkhouse, and across the yard were three smaller structures which would be a wagonshed, a smokehouse and probably a blacksmith shop.

'Looks like a real nice lay-out,' he reflected.

Susan said proudly, 'It is. And it's worth fighting for.'

Beauregarde was thinking about those words an hour later when he spread his blankets in the bunkhouse and crawled into them. Susan Blake, he decided, was a fitting daughter for an arrogant old warhorse who would fight to the last ditch and die in it before he'd consider surrender.

So thinking, Beauregarde went to sleep and for the first time in years dreamed about a girl—a girl with honey-hued hair and sweet-curving lips and the bluest eyes he had ever seen . . .

★   ★   ★

During the next four days Lee Beauregarde learned a lot about Panamint Valley and the people who lived in it. The first morning Dave Blake had ridden with him to the bald crest of Skyline Ridge, which was fifteen miles southwest of Three Links. From this high vantage point Blake had reported the exact location of each ranch in the valley.

'Over east there is Paddock's Boxed P,' the old cowman had directed. 'A little north of him, hard by the base of that mesa, is Tate Corvette's TC, and just west of him, in that next canyon, is Hank Lundermann's Lazy L. Off south and east is Jeb Hodnett's Spear H, and that smoke you see in the hills above it is coming from Ellison's O Bar E.'

Then Blake had swung his pointing finger to the south, where a hazy blur of buildings showed against the sun-hammered flats. 'That's the Skillet,' he said bluntly. 'Strebor controls everything from there to the Border.'

After that initial excursion, Beauregarde had set out alone each morning, riding long circles that kept him in the saddle until late afternoon. Except for the time it took him to eat his meals, he stayed away from the main house, and therefore saw little of Susan. But though he guarded the fact well, his admiration for her grew with each day's passing. The meals she prepared were the best he'd ever eaten, and she kept the big house in immaculate condition . . .

Then, on the fifth day, Beauregarde met Cliff Paddock riding through the timber in the Dragoon Hills. It was entirely casual, that meeting. They were headed in opposite directions on one of the numerous cattle trails that crisscrossed the region.

Greeting him in friendly fashion, Paddock halted his big sorrel stallion abreast of Beauregarde and produced a sack of Durham.

'Smoke?' he invited.

Beauregarde accepted and, reaching for the tobacco noticed the ring on the little finger of Paddock's extended hand. It was an oddly shaped cameo and there was a bluish thread caught under one claw. Finished with the tobacco, Beauregarde returned it, saying, 'Much obliged.'

'Everything seems quiet as all git-out,'

Paddock declared complainingly.

Remembering that Susan Blake was scheduled to marry this man, Beauregarde placed a tentative significance on his words, and tried again to tally his pedigree.

'Too quiet for you?' he asked.

'Hell, yes. If trouble has to come, I'd like to see it come quick—and get it over with the same way.'

Beauregarde watched Paddock shape up a cigarette. This blocky, brown-eyed rider had an indolent way with him. He seemed thoroughly relaxed at all times, without worry or wariness. It was, Beauregarde decided, the way a man should be, especially a young man. Recognizing these traits in Cliff Paddock, he felt the beginnings of envy. Paddock he reflected, had reason to be good-natured and relaxed. He had a place of his own, and a girl who would one day share it . . .

Yet despite this reasoning and the logic that accompanied it, Beauregarde sensed a quality in Paddock that he couldn't tab; something that didn't quite fit the frame of the Boxed P owner's genial air of frankness and straightforward talk. Beauregarde was toying with that evasive flaw in Paddock's makeup when they went their separate ways. He was still toying with it as he rode up to the Three Links corral and saw Susan standing with her father beside the Ellisons' wagon. The rig was piled high with furniture, and Della Ellison seemed to be sobbing.

Almost at once Dave Blake strode over to the corral. 'It's started,' he reported grimly. 'By God, they burned 'em out.'

Beauregarde watched Susan escort Mrs. Ellison into the house; and even with the import of Blake's words rifling through him, his mind registered the way Susan's hair shone like burnished copper in the sunlight.

'Skillet framed up a brand-blotching trick on Oscar,' Blake continued. 'Strebor's new foreman and three men rode into Ellison's yard this morning with the hide of a fresh-killed steer. The Skillet brand had been worked over into Oscar's O Bar E. They made a big talk about Pool members rustling from Strebor and how they was taking the law into their own hands on account of Sheriff Derbyshire refusing to protect Skillet's interests. They gave Oscar one hour to pack up his belongings, and then they set fire to his house.'

'An old game,' Beauregarde reflected, remembering all the times it had been played in Texas. 'It gives Strebor an excuse for a freezeout play.'

Blake scowled, and said, 'You take it mighty cool and collected. You talk like burning a man's home was an everyday affair.'

'It may be, from now on,' Beauregarde said dryly, and eased over to where Ellison was unhitching his team.

The yellow-haired young cowman was tight-lipped and bleak-eyed. He looked like a man without hope . . .

'Any idea when the brand trick was played?' Beauregarde asked.

Ellison didn't look up. He unhooked the trace chains and said grimly, 'The blotch was fresh, not more than one day old. It was a botchy piece of work.'

'Always is, when it's part of a frameup,' Beauregarde said. 'Don't suppose you located the carcass.'

Ellison shook his head. Whereupon Beauregarde went into the corral and roped a fresh horse. 'I'm going to take a look-see around,' he informed Blake.

★ ★ ★

Two hours of riding brought Lee Beauregarde to the edge of the O Bar E yard shortly before sundown. There he halted, looking at the charred wreckage which had so recently been a house. Guessing that Della Ellison had taken a young wife's pride in giving her place a homelike atmosphere, Beauregarde conjured up a picture of how it had looked. There'd probably been bright curtains in the windows, pretty paper borders on the shelves, and a score of little things a woman's hands could contrive to turn a house into a home.

Now only ashes remained. This smouldering heap was a symbol of Sid Strebor's lust for land, and because Beauregarde could put an accurate reckoning on such things, he knew there'd soon be other symbols—blood stains on the brush, bullet-blasted bodies sprawled in lonely arroyos. There'd be weeping women and grim-faced men and crying kids before this thing was ended. For that was the inevitable warp and woof of range war and it seldom varied . . .

Gazing at the mound of ashes brought back a bitter memory of his flame-gutted shack in Texas. It made him recall the dismal day he'd ridden into his own yard and picked up his father's battered hat near another heap of smouldering embers. He had stood there on that occasion, turning the hat brim in his hands, looking at the irregular pattern of sweat stains on the band, and thinking how like Jeff Beauregarde that frayed fabric was—wrinkled and gray and marked by long years of faithful service. Then he'd stepped over to the lifeless form and gently placed the hat on his father's death-blanched face.

Vividly recalling that scene now, Beauregarde sat gripped in the clutch of long-festering hatred for the man who'd killed his father. Three years hadn't dulled the sharpness of that hatred, nor the black memory of its birth. He had stood there in the yard staring down at the two red-rimmed holes in old Jeff's shirt, just above the buckle of his horsehair belt, and at the pool of congealing blood on the ground. Old Jeff, who had liked to ride fast with the wind in his face, had died slowly in gut-shot agony.

Then finally he'd noticed something that had sent him to his knees, something that had put a questing glint in his tear-wet eyes. For there, traced in the dust by a wavering finger, had been seven crudely formed letters—R O B E R T S. Staring at those stark symbols, Lee Beauregarde had sworn a vow of vengeance; he had dedicated his gun to retribution. Three long years ago—

Remembering all that now, Beauregarde rode slowly across the O Bar E yard to where the hide of a line-backed grulla steer hung on the corral gate. The Skillet part of the brand had been reburned with an upright and two horizontal lines added to the handle in a way that made an O Bar E. The burning, which had obviously been done a day or two before, was crudely handled. Something about the hide seemed vaguely familiar—but Beauregarde couldn't identify

59

the reason. Perhaps, he thought, he'd seen this line-backed steer during one of his jaunts through the hills.

Beauregarde took a turn around the yard, picked up the incoming hoof prints of the four Skillet riders and was back-tracking that sign with the intention of finding the steer's carcass when he glimpsed a horseman riding toward him. For a moment, with the sun's slanting rays in his eyes, Beauregarde was unable to identify the rider. Acting on pure impulse, he reined sharply to the left, this move placing the other man on his gun side.

It was an owlhoot maneuver, and—because it automatically shielded the brand side of his horse—was against the etiquette of the trail. But Lee Beauregarde had long since discarded the careless habits of peaceable men. Hand hovering close to gun butt, he peered through the sun glare with a questing, tight-eyed wariness . . .

Until Sheriff Sam Derbyshire called, 'Howdy, Beauregarde.'

Then all the cocked tension went out of Beauregarde and he said, 'Looks like you're a trifle late, friend. The damage has all been done.'

Derbyshire pulled up, muttering morosely. 'I saw the smoke and rode over to investigate. Met up with the Skillet bunch, who said they just burned out a rustler. They showed me the carcass of a steer they'd skinned. I was just riding in for a look at the hide.'

'It's there all right,' Beauregarde reported. 'A Skillet burned into an O Bar E so plain you could spot it five miles away. Whoever did it must've used a crowbar for a running iron.'

Derbyshire dug out a plug of chewing tobacco and gnawed at it reflectively. 'Funny thing,' he mused. 'A damned funny thing. Never figgered young Oscar was a long looper. He never seemed overly ambitious thataway.'

Those words startled Beauregarde. The thought that Ellison had actually done the brand blotching hadn't occurred to him. He asked surprisedly: 'You got any doubts about its being a Skillet frameup?'

'I didn't have, at first,' Derbyshire admitted. 'Not until I'd spent four hours circling the fire where that steer's brand was altered. I still can't figger why Oscar should turn into a cow thief, him always bein' so honest and married to a sweet wife like he is. But I'm satisfied *no Skillet rider did the job.*'

'Why?' Beauregarde demanded.

Derbyshire thoughtfully squirted tobacco juice into the dirt. He wiped his mouth and stared off toward the hills, apparently reluctant to talk. There was something peculiar here, Beauregarde realized; something that didn't make sense. Why, he asked himself, should Sheriff Derbyshire be so damned sure no Skillet rider had blotched that brand? How *could* he be so sure?

He asked again, 'What makes you think it wasn't the Skillet?'

'Well,' the sheriff said, 'I did a mess of looking. Like I just said, I spent four hours looking—which means I covered considerable ground. The man that blotched that brand rode in from the north. Except for the fresh sign of those four riders this morning, there ain't another set of tracks runnin' toward the Skillet that could've been made in over a week. By God, that's one thing I'm sure of, and it's about the only thing.'

The flogging rhythm of a running horse turned them both in saddle. Derbyshire said, 'Somebody else comin' for a look-see. There'll be plenty o' fast riding and plenty o' looking in this country from now on.'

Then Susan Blake rode through a mesquite thicket and set her horse back on its haunches. Ignoring Beauregarde, she faced the sheriff and asked, 'What do you think of the Skillet bunch today? Don't you think it's about time you took sides with the decent people in this valley, Sam?'

Beauregarde saw the impact of those words register plainly on the old lawman's craggy face. Derbyshire's features tightened into a frown and he muttered, 'Long as I'm wearing this here badge, I'm taking no sides.'

'But what about that burned house over there?' Susan demanded. 'Isn't that something you can side against?'

There was an arrogance in her voice now; a domineering glint in her unsmiling eyes. And in that moment Lee Beauregarde understood why Dave Blake's face had seemed familiar that night in the Silver Dollar Saloon. At times like this, with anger, clouding her face and arrogance riding her voice, Susan bore a striking resemblance to her father . . .

'The Skillet seems to have a fair case against Ellison,' Derbyshire said patiently. 'The evidence shows somebody worked a Skillet into an O Bar E.'

Instant amazement came into Susan's voice. 'Are you trying to tell me you have any doubts that this is just a sneaking frameup?' she exclaimed.

'Yes,' Derbyshire said. 'That's exactly what I'm telling you, Susie. No Skillet rider blotched that brand. Either Oscar got too ambitious, or I'm blind as a bat when it comes to reading signs.'

'You *are* blind!' Susan insisted heatedly. 'You're blind to everything except the one thing you should overlook. Can't you understand that the time for fair legal action is past in this country? Can't you see it's just a fight between honest men and crooks?'

Then she turned to Beauregarde and said, 'Dad wants you to ride with me to spread the word there's going to be a Pool meeting at our place tomorrow. He wants every member to be present.'

She spurred her bronc and quartered through the brush.

Beauregarde gave Derbyshire a farewell salute and followed her. When he'd caught up she said briefly, 'We'll go to the Boxed P first.'

She led the way in silence, the frowning set of her sunlit face showing how strongly she resented Derbyshire's refusal to side the Pool. She didn't speak until they dropped into a canyon where a one-room shack perched forlornly on a boulder strewn slope.

Cliff Paddock stood in the doorway, and Susan said to Beauregarde, 'He'll be glad to hear we're going to fight at last. He wanted the Pool to tackle Skillet three months ago, when Strebor first started crowding the grass.'

Presently they pulled up in front of the shack, and Paddock called, 'Light down and rest your saddles.'

When Susan told him the news and that Blake wanted the Pool members at Three Links tomorrow, Paddock grinned, 'Mebbe now we'll have some action,' he declared. 'I'm sorry Oscar's tough luck had to be the thing to bring it, but I'm glad we're going to have a showdown.'

Then he added thoughtfully, 'I don't like the idea of you riding around this country now, honey, even with a six-gun smokeroo for an escort.'

Beauregarde searched Paddock's face for a sign of malice. But there was none there, nor in his voice.

'I'll be all right,' Susan declared. 'I've got to get the word around.'

But Paddock shook his head. 'I'll notify the folks. You ride back to the ranch and stay there until this thing is finished.'

Without hesitation Susan agreed to that arrangement, and it was this instant acquiescence to Paddock's decision which caused Beauregarde to smile secretively as they rode back out of the canyon.

'When,' he inquired, 'is the ceremony going to take place?'

They were riding at a walk, close enough for him to see the change in her eyes. 'What makes you ask that?' she inquired.

For a moment their glances met and held, and Lee Beauregarde sensed again the rich qualities of this girl who so obviously disliked him, or disliked his kind.

'Well,' he drawled, 'that time I said you'd better ride on, the day we met, you told me you rode as you pleased. But you didn't tell

65

Paddock that. So I figger you'll be taking all your orders from him directly.'

The logic of his reasoning brought a smile to Susan's lips, and in that moment she seemed more beautiful than she'd ever seemed. Her eyes were warmer, and her voice held a tone close to comradeship when she said, 'You're a strange man, Lee Beauregarde. You don't say much, but you do a deal of thinking.'

'That doesn't answer my question,' he prompted, hugely enjoying this personal conversation.

Whereupon she peered up at him the way she had that day on the flats. And as on that day, he sensed the womanliness in this girl which revived memories of long forgotten pleasures; memories of a time when life was gay and richly flavored and well worth the living.

'Your interest,' she murmured, 'is highly flattering. Especially for a girl with no more warmth than winter sun on a snowdrift.'

So she had remembered! The knowledge that she'd retained that first, hasty judgment which he'd so swiftly reconstructed pleased him more than he'd been pleased in many a month. 'I was wrong about that,' he admitted. 'I changed my opinion within a couple of minutes.'

'In what way?' she asked archly.

'I saw you were proud instead of haughty,'

he explained. 'I saw there was real warmth in your eyes, and you had the pride that good breeding puts into a woman.'

It was almost dark now, but Beauregarde glimpsed the quick pennants of color which warmed her cheeks.

'My—what sharp eyes you had that day,' she murmured mockingly. 'Was that all you saw, Mister Beauregarde?'

She was close to him—closer than she should have been. So close that the perfume of her hair was a deliciously pleasing scent in his nostrils—a subtle, feminine scent intimate and arousing. Propelled by an urge he couldn't resist, Beauregarde reached over and pulled her toward him. He said huskily, 'Yes, I saw something else. I saw you were the most beautiful woman in the world.'

For one breathless instant he teetered on the verge of kissing the exclamation from her protesting lips. Then abruptly he released her, and watched the instinctive way her slim fingers reached up to tuck back a tumbled strand of hair . . .

'Is—is that why you herded your red-haired friend away from me?' she asked accusingly, her voice plainly showing emotional stress. 'Was it because you wanted to force your own attentions on me?'

It was, Beauregarde knew, a fair question. She had a right to judge him now—to place him in the same calico-chasing class with Red Valentine. He sought for words to correct that impression; to tell her how he really felt. But because he couldn't comprehend the urgency of his own impulses and desires he had no words to explain them.

So he said briefly, 'I didn't intend to do that, ma'am.'

'I've heard that Hades is paved with good intentions,' she murmured, and rode on ahead of him. But later, when they unsaddled at the corral, she asked, 'Are you still wondering when the ceremony is going to take place?'

That question, and the comradely tone of her voice, caught Beauregarde completely unprepared. Confusion disrupted the orderly procession of his thoughts, and for a moment he stood speechless. She had every right to dislike him now, yet she was being friendly. And in this interval of astonishment Red Valentine's smirking declaration came to him—'Them fancy ones ain't no different from the others,' Red had said: 'They all like a little sweetenin' now and then!'

He said finally, 'Reckon it was none of my business, ma'am.'

'It wasn't,' she agreed, 'but I'll tell you anyway.'

Then she ceased speaking as Dave Blake called from the lighted doorway, 'What's up?

Why you back so soon?'

'Cliff is making the ride,' Susan called back to him. 'Cliff said he didn't want me gadding around the country.'

Blake grunted something unintelligible, then asked, 'Wasn't Beauregarde with you?'

'Yes—but Cliff didn't think it was safe.'

Beauregarde said quietly, 'Guess you agree with Paddock about that.'

Whereupon Susan chuckled. 'That depends on what he wants me protected from,' she announced, and went quickly across the yard.

CHAPTER THREE

Afterward, while Susan and Della Ellison washed the supper dishes, Beauregarde sat with Blake and Oscar on the gallery. The talk at the table had been all on one subject—how Pool members would react to the ruthlessness of the Skillet's first blow. And that question was the topic of conversation now.

'We'd planned to fight a defensive war,' Blake muttered, a plain note of worry in his voice. 'We figgered we could keep Strebor from crowding us by chousing his stuff off our range and keeping it off. But it's too late for that now. Strebor isn't going to dillydally around; he's going to knock all the fight out of us quick—unless we stop him.'

Remembering the cool way Mrs. Hodnett had looked at him that night in Apache Tank, and the lack of enthusiasm with which Tate Corvette had greeted him, Beauregarde guessed why Blake was worried. Faced with the grim necessity of discarding a defensive form of fighting, Blake was wondering if his fellow members would take to the idea of reprisal warfare—if they'd have the guts to go it whole hog, root or die . . .

'You figgering to attack the Skillet?' Beauregarde inquired.

'That's the only thing left for us to do,' Blake declared sternly. 'We've got to smash the Skillet before it smashes us. If we sit around and wait, it won't be long before Strebor's riffraff will find a Skillet cow with its brand worked into a Spear H, or a Lazy W. Then another house will be burned.'

Oscar Ellison asked moodily, 'Suppose we don't cut the mustard. Suppose Strebor's bunch stands us off. What then?'

'It'll be dog eat dog and the devil take the hindermost,' Blake prophesied. 'But if we fight it to a finish right now we'll have a good chance to win. The Skillet ain't so damn strong but what it can be whupped, and we ain't so weak but what we can do the whupping.'

Beauregarde asked, 'You think all your members will stick with the Pool when they

70

hear what it's going to be?' and knew at once that he'd hit a target of doubt in Blake's mind.

The old cowman didn't answer for a moment. He tamped a load of tobacco into his pipe and then forgot to light it. Finally he admitted, 'That's what I'm worrying about. Cliff Paddock has been trying to talk 'em into a showdown fight for weeks. But Jeb Hodnett and Tate Corvette were against it, or their wives were—which is the same thing. Hank Lundermann hasn't got a wife. He's willing to do anything that don't interfere with his likker. But we've got to have every member with us if we're goin' to cut the mustard.'

For a reason he couldn't identify, Beauregarde had an urge to ride. He said, 'Guess I'll take a little pasear in the hills.'

'You think there's something to see up there?' Blake asked quickly, the tone of his voice showing how on edge he was.

'No, it's just a notion,' Beauregarde admitted, 'and a way of earning my wages.'

Whereupon he sauntered across to the corral and, saddling a horse, rode up the slants behind Three Links. Reaching the rim of Horseshoe Mesa, he turned for a look at the ranch below and sat for a moment, idly watching the kitchen window's square of illumination blink on and off as one of the girls walked between lamp and window.

A slight breeze stirred the greasewood into

a gentle sighing, but save for that the night's deep hush was undisturbed. Following the rimrock for a mile or so, Beauregarde drifted down into the valley by leisurely stages and headed southward. There was no definite purpose in his ride, nor any set destination. The urge to prowl had been prompted by Dave Blake's talk of impending conflict, and by a subtle premonition that nagged him with the need for movement.

Presently his bronc angled into a well-grooved trail which Beauregarde guessed ran between Tate Corvette's place and the Lazy L. And because Blake had referred to young Pike Corvette's courtship of Judy Lundermann, Beauregarde smiled reflectively. Some things never changed. Come storm or strife, there'd always been galoots who'd ride long miles to 'go a' galin' ' and there always would be. Romance, he guessed, had cut more trails across the west than commerce ever would.

Topping a wooded knoll, he was halted by the sound of nearby voices. A man said, 'Good night, honey—I'll see you at Three Links tomorrow.'

There was a creak of saddle leather and then a girl's low-toned: 'Good night, Pike.'

Beauregarde grinned. If this was all the darkness shielded in the way of night riders, he might better be getting his rest. He was on the point of turning back when Pike Corvette came trotting toward him and his horse nickered a greeting.

'Who's that?' the young rider demanded worriedly.

Beauregarde identified himself, explaining, 'Just riding south for a look-see.'

Corvette pulled alongside, 'I heard about your fight with Buck Casco,' he said. 'Sure wish I'd been in town to see it, Mister Beauregarde.'

In the momentary silence that followed he added, 'Guess I'd better hit a shuck for home. Got to bust out of the blankets early in the morning.'

He rode on, and Beauregarde was wondering if Judy Lunderman had also departed, when she asked cheerfully, 'Riding my way, Texican?'

The plain invitation in her low-pitched voice surprised Beauregarde. Her voice held the cadenced richness of a woman's voice—that voice of a gracious, emotional woman. And in that moment, before he replied, Beauregarde remembered another thing Dave Blake had said about Judy Lundermann—'She grew up with a booze-guzzling father and two scamp brothers who lined out for the gold fields a year ago. Judy is ten years older than her age.'

The hoof beat of Corvette's bronc had diminished to a remote murmur of sound when Beauregarde said, 'No, ma'am. I was

73

just making a circle.'

She was little more than a deeper shadow against the night's unbroken gloom, yet the sense of her presence came strongly across the dark. And when she spoke again her voice was like a hand reaching out to touch him—a seductive, caressing hand.

'Won't you ride a little way with me,' she urged, 'just for company?'

Beauregarde chuckled. She had a way with her, this daughter of big Hank Lundermann—a damned appealing way. She made a man remember half-forgotten pleasures. He said, 'Sure,' and they rode close enough so that their stirrups touched as they went along the trail.

'Are you going to be at the Pool meeting tomorrow?' she inquired.

'Reckon so,' Beauregarde said.

Whereupon she exclaimed in a thoroughly pleased voice, 'Then I'll get to see you in daylight. This is the second time I've seen you at night—but I can't see you at all now. I'm wondering about your eyes. I'd like to know if they're blue or gray.'

That frank admission startled Beauregarde, and somehow pleased him. He asked, 'Which color do you prefer?'

'Gray. Are yours that color?'

'Don't know, exactly. Most of the mirrors I've looked into were downright dusty.'

That brought a ripple of amusement and the assertion: 'You men are all alike.' Then she added thoughtfully, 'You're different than most, though. I knew that the first time I saw you.'

Which was a puzzle Beauregarde couldn't solve.

They had reached the east side of the knoll now, and the Lazy L's lights glowed at the base of it. 'Reckon this is far as I go,' Beauregarde said, and was turning away when she reached out and plucked at his sleeve.

'Maybe I shouldn't tell you this,' she murmured, 'but I think you ought to know. Pike says his mother thinks it's wrong for the Pool to hire a professional gunslinger, and Mrs. Hodnett agrees with her.'

'So?' Beauregarde muttered, instantly recognizing the importance of her information. If his presence on the Pool payroll was already causing dissension, then Dave Blake's plan for attacking Skillet might stir up a veritable hornet's nest of opposition at tomorrow's meeting . . .

'I don't agree with them at all,' Judy declared. 'I'm glad Dave Blake hired you.'

She released her hold on his sleeve, and riding on down the slope, called teasingly, 'I'm sure your eyes are gray, Texican.'

Beauregarde grinned and continued southward. Judy's report had reminded him of

Blake's declared intention of waging war on the Skillet. Now it occurred to him that it might be wise to scout Strebor's stronghold; to learn how well Strebor was organized against attack.

With that idea in mind, Beauregarde rode through the tumbled hills south of the Lazy L and later, when the land leveled off, urged his horse to a faster pace. This trip might not produce a single shred of useful information; it might be futile as many another ride had been. But though the outcome of the fight between the Skillet and the Pool held no personal interest for him nor hope of profit, there was a deep-rooted integrity in Beauregarde which made him want to earn his wages. Anything he could learn to-night might pay dividends when the Pool rode against the Skillet. And if Dave Blake had his way, that would be soon—very soon!

Presently Beauregarde picked up the Skillet's lights and for upwards of an hour loped toward them across a level, almost brushless plain. The lights were still half a mile away when a rider emerged from the gloom ahead and challenged, 'That you, Gregg?'

Beauregarde pulled to a stop, and for a moment, while he identified that voice as Faro Savoy's, he kept silent. Then it occurred to him that this tubercular gunhawk wouldn't be too well acquainted with the voices of Skillet riders. So he muttered, 'Yes,' and rode directly

76

toward Savoy's vague shape.

'Anything stirring up north?' Savoy inquired.

Beauregarde said, 'No.'

The presence of a sentry that far from Skillet headquarters showed how craftily Sid Strebor was organized against a surprise attack from revenge-prodded Pool members. It was a valuable thing to know . . .

Riding so close to Savoy that he could have reached out and touched the reedy rider, Beauregarde muttered, 'Reckon I'll mosey on in.'

There was a moment then when he thought he was going to get away with it. But in the next instant Savoy demanded suspiciously, 'Say—you don't talk like Gregg. Who the hell are you?'

★   ★   ★

Beauregarde was passing on the left, this wary habit giving him all the best of it, when he lifted his gun and, leaning close, brought the weapon's barrel down hard on Savoy's steeple-crowned sombrero. Savoy uttered a rasping exclamation that was half cough, half grunt. Then he slid from the far side of his saddle, and that clumsy fall sent his bronc crowding against Beauregarde.

'Steady,' Beauregarde coaxed, and

endeavored to grasp the animal's dangling reins. But the thudding impact of Savoy's body spooked the bronc into a tantrum; it lunged past Beauregarde in snorting panic and went galloping across the flats.

Beauregarde cursed. That bronc would circle home, and its arrival would be a tip-off to Savoy's mishap. Hurriedly dismounting, Beauregarde ran his hands over Savoy's sprawled form, found Faro's gun and drew it from its holster. The blow on the head, he guessed, hadn't been hard enough to do permanent damage; Savoy would soon recover consciousness—but he would have no gun to attract attention.

Tossing the weapon far into the darkness, Beauregarde climbed into the saddle and headed straight for the Skillet's lights. This excursion was turning out better than he'd anticipated. Already it had given him an opportunity to repay Savoy for that sneak shot from the rear door of the Silver Dollar; perhaps he'd reap some further benefit . . .

When he was within a quarter mile of the Skillet yard, Beauregarde slowed his bronc to a walk. A bit farther he rode into a deep arroyo and followed this defile for a short distance before finding a suitable place to climb out of it. When he topped the opposite bank he was so close to the ranch yard that he halted instantly.

Long fingers of yellow lamplight reached out from the windows of two buildings. In front of the larger structure a saddled horse stood slack-hipped in the doorway's shaft of lamplight; nearby, but in the shadows, Beauregarde discerned the vague shapes of two men.

Prompted by a growing sense of curiosity, Beauregarde dismounted, tied his bronc to a clump of greasewood and moved cautiously toward the house. There were no lighted windows on this side, yet because the darkness which shielded his approach might also shield a waiting sentinel, Beauregarde halted for a momentary probing of the roundabout shadows.

High-riding clouds blanketed out the stars. A stronger breeze was blowing from the north, warmer and with a warning of rain in its sultry dampness. The rumor of hoofbeats came faintly along the breeze, that sound reminding Beauregarde of Savoy's loose horse, and telling him how short a time he had to scout this place . . .

Moving quickly forward, Beauregarde reached a row of dwarfed pepper trees that bordered the south side of the yard. There he halted briefly, listening to an unintelligible drone of voices emanating from the farther building which he tallied as a bunkhouse. Then he stepped quickly across the yard and, reaching the main building's wall, eased along it to the front corner. He heard Sid Strebor's sharp-toned voice.

'Sure,' the Skillet owner declared. 'Sure I will. I've got nothing to lose.'

Cigar smoke sent a fragrant aroma across the darkness. For a moment those yonderly men were silent, and in that interval Beauregarde's mind registered the fact that the drifting hoofbeats were plainer now. If that oncoming horse was Savoy's, this would be a poor place to linger. A very poor place!

Then the other man spoke and, recognizing that voice as belonging to Sheriff Derbyshire, Beauregarde was completely surprised. What, he wondered, was the old lawman doing there? What possible reason could he have for holding a night conference with Sid Strebor?

'We'll give it a whirl,' the lawman said. 'Chances are he'd be out of jail soon as a jury could reach a verdict. But I want this country to know there's more to law and order than just one man's opinion.'

The discovery that Derbyshire was discussing law and order with Skillet's range-grabbing boss baffled Beauregarde. It was ironical—almost laughable—that a peace officer should stand there calmly philosophizing about legal procedure with a man who was directly responsible for the burning of another man's home . . .

Added to that puzzle was another. What, Beauregarde wondered, did Derbyshire mean by his talk of jails and juries; and who was he referring to? Certainly not Oscar Ellison, on a charge of rustling. Even though the sheriff had seemed strangely undecided about Ellison's guilt, he wouldn't arrest him after what Strebor's riders had done. Or would he?

'Maybe we'll find a way to keep him in jail,' Strebor snapped. 'Or put him out of circulation entirely.'

Derbyshire said, 'I don't know about that,' and then ceased speaking as a man called across the yard, 'Riderless horse just showed up at the corral!'

'Whose is it?' Strebor demanded, instantly alert.

'Don't know, but it's carryin' your brand.'

'Find out!' Strebor ordered impatiently. 'Find out damned quick, you fool!'

Beauregarde eased back along the wall. This was drawing it a bit too fine. Strebor's suspicions were already aroused; once the full significance of that riderless horse struck the Skillet boss, he'd throw a dragnet of riders around the yard and there'd be no possible chance of escape . . .

Wind-blown rain spattered against Beauregarde's face as he started back across the yard. He'd taken a dozen steps when he heard Red Valentine yell,

'By God, it's Savoy's bronc! Somebody got in close enough to git Faro!'

Quickly then Beauregarde ran across the yard, his footfalls muffled by the sandy soil and by the increasing patter of rain. But quiet as his movement was, it wasn't without sound, and Sid Strebor evidently detected it, for he shouted, 'Out here—out here!'

That snarled summons was instantly punctuated by the slash of a close-flying slug—by a great hullabaloo of voices and the merged explosions of blasting guns. Beauregarde increased his stride and, reaching his horse, hastily mounted and rode into the arroyo.

Bullets were lacing the air above him as his horse slid down the steep, already rain-soaked bank. The searching lead made a wickedly rustling sound against the breeze-blown rain; it plunked into the opposite, higher bank and showed Beauregarde how surely those yonder gunmen had spotted him.

The rain was slanting down in gusty sheets now, turning this arroyo into a hock-deep stream. And because he understood how fatal it would be to get bogged in that muddy trough, Beauregarde decided against following it farther north. Better, he thought, to take a chance on random slugs now than to be caught later in a slaughter chute. So thinking, he booted his bronc up the opposite bank and grinned because the Skillet bunch were still directing their lead toward the spot where he'd slid into the arroyo.

But a moment later, as his horse crashed through a mesquite thicket, Beauregarde's grin faded entirely. A thrusting branch ripped his carbine scabbard from the saddle, and the crackle of breaking brush had attracted Skillet's attention. Bullets were spattering mud all about him now, but because the Henry carbine and scabbard had been a gift from his dead father, Lee Beauregarde halted his horse and, dismounting, retrieved the fallen gungear.

When he climbed back into the saddle a random slug sizzled so close that it spooked the bronc into a fit of bucking that almost unseated Beauregarde. But because each added escape added to his sense of exhilaration, Beauregarde didn't cuss out the bronc; and later, when he saw a group of horsemen stream across the Skillet's lamplit yard, Beauregarde loosed a reckless, taunting laugh. Strebor's bunch had taken too much time getting saddles on their horses; they'd been so eager to cut him down that they'd allowed him to ride out of range before getting mounted.

Orange flashes of muzzle-flame spurted weirdly through the rain. But all the slugs of that yonder shooting were falling far short now. Beauregarde laughed again and lined out for the Dragoon Hills. He had penetrated the

Skillet's sentry line and learned something of Strebor's plans, and because he had happened to tie his horse at the edge of an arroyo he was going to live to tell about those plans . . .

His luck, he reflected, might run out eventually. But it wasn't running out tonight!

★   ★   ★

Lee Beauregarde was sitting in the wagonshed doorway mending his damaged carbine scabbard when Hank Lundermann and Judy rode into the Three Links yard shortly after breakfast. The big cowman slouched carelessly in the saddle, his appearance seeming the more shiftless in contrast with that of the trim, fresh-faced girl at his side.

He called, 'Mornin', Beauregarde,' that lusty-voiced greeting bringing Dave Blake and Susan out to the gallery.

Beauregarde waved, and watched the pair of fathers and daughters meet on the gallery steps. There was, he reflected, as much difference between the men as there was in the two girls. Blake, stiffly erect for all his fifty-odd years, was honed to a flinty hardness that kept him lean of girth and sharp of eye. The difference showed also in the faces of these two: Blake's features bearing the plain stamp of a dominant, prideful man—Lundermann's face slack and indifferent and blotched by long years of heavy drinking.

The two girls were well matched as to size, both medium tall and moulded in the way a woman should be. But the likeness ended there, for Judy Lundermann was as graphically brunette as Susan was blonde. Judy's eyes, Beauregarde guessed, were either black or dark brown. She was gazing his way; remembering her talk last night, Beauregarde wondered if she was trying to tally the color of his eyes now . . .

Oscar Ellison came out onto the gallery, and presently the girls went inside. Beauregarde continued with his mending, wanting this scabbard to be in perfect working order. A man never knew when he'd have need for his saddle gun; he was pondering the probabilities of needing it soon, when the TC wagon rolled in from the brush with Tate Corvette perched insignificantly on the seat beside as large a woman as Lee Beauregarde had ever seen.

Four youngsters, ranging in size from a little girl with blue ribbons in her hair to a freckle-faced stripling of early 'teenage, in the wagon box. Directly behind the rig rode Pike Corvette, looking slick in his Sunday hat and scarlet silk arm bands and hand-tooled boots. The Corvettes were merging with the group on the gallery when Jeb Hodnett and Cliff Paddock rode into the yard, their arrival completing the Pool membership.

Watching all this, and thoroughly comprehending its meaning, Beauregarde fell into a reflective mood. Here were all the ingredients of life and love and happiness. Yet, here also were the makings of tragedy—of death and hate and heartbreak. Faced by threat of impending conflict, these folks were gathered in a common cause. They were a unit now, and because there was strength in unity, they were quite confident. But homes couldn't be corraled into a compact group; homes were scattered, isolated by miles of open country. Ranches couldn't be defended as a unit, and therein lay the Pool's chief weakness. The Skillet could swoop down on them one by one and, using the pretext of ridding the range of cow-stealing families, could clear them all out in one month's time.

The vital importance of that line of reasoning came up for discussion a few minutes later when the men gathered in the bunkhouse for a council of war.

Dave Blake opened the confab with a grim report of the O Bar E burn-out. Repeating what Sheriff Derbyshire had told Susan, he added angrily, 'That shows how much backing we can expect from the pussyfooting old woman we voted into office. Derbyshire not only refuses to side us—he's calling us cow thieves!'

'It looks like Sam's gittin' spooky in his old

age,' Jeb Hodnett reflected. 'Seems like his reasonin' has gone haywire for a fact. If the Skillet didn't do that brand fixin', who in hell would've done it?'

Lundermann grinned at Oscar Ellison, and said jokingly, 'Guess Sam has the deadwood on you at last, kid.'

Seeing the way Ellison flushed, not bothering to defend himself, Beauregarde made a mental note that Derbyshire was wrong in his guess of Ellison's guilt. The O Bar E owner had none of the characteristics of a greedy man, nor of an overly ambitious builder of a big cow spread. He looked like a mild-mannered youngster dumbfounded by the turn events had taken.

But if Ellison was innocent, and the sign showed that no Skillet rider could have done the job, who had done it? And why?

Which was when Beauregarde's mind grasped at a devious angle in the game. Suppose a member of the Pool was in cahoots with Skillet, working under cover for high pay? And in that same moment Beauregarde remembered the open-handed way Hank Lundermann had ordered up the drinks that night in the Silver Dollar . . .

Cliff Paddock said, 'Wonder who Skillet will tie into next.'

That quietly spoken wedge of words brought an interval of silence. It was

87

as if each man there were weighing his own chances, visualizing what would happen with the dreaded appearance of Sid Strebor's house-burning brigade.

All except Hank Lundermann, who broke the hush with a chuckle. 'Mebbe it'll be me,' he prophesied. 'It would be a brass-riveted cinch to change my Lazy L into a Skillet.'

'Most any brand can be worked into a Skillet, if you ain't particular what it looks like,' Blake snapped. 'From what Beauregarde tells me, Strebor ain't particular about his brand-blotting.'

'If there was only some way we could know where the Skillet was going to strike next,' Tate Corvette said wishfully.

And Jeb Hodnett muttered, 'Yeah—then we could be set and waiting' on 'em. And we could give Strebor's wild bunch a run for their money, by grab!'

Hank Lundermann grunted agreement to that. He said, 'What we need is a spy in Strebor's camp.'

He glanced at Beauregarde then and asked, 'How about them two drifters you rode into town with the other day? Couldn't you talk one of 'em into tippin' us off to Strebor's plans ahead of time?'

This talk of spies added fresh fuel to the embers of Beauregarde's frugal suspicion. It could be coincidence, of course, but it seemed

88

strange that Lundermann should be the one to bring up the subject of spies. It showed a craftiness that didn't seem to fit Hank Lundermann's slipshod, easy-going ways . . .

Beauregarde said, 'No, I guess not. Red Valentine is rodding Strebor's crew, and Faro Savoy hates my guts.'

'To hell with spies,' Dave Blake said impatiently. 'We know all we need to know about the Skillet. After what happened yesterday, it don't take no spy to tell us what Strebor plans to do, and what we've got to do to stop him. There's only one way to make Panamint Valley a safe place to live in—and that's to smash Skillet clean off the range!'

Beauregarde watched the impact of that declaration register on those roundabout faces. Cliff Paddock smiled, plainly agreeing with Blake. But there was no smile on Tate Corvette's face; the crotchety little rancher glanced soberly at Jeb Hodnett, meeting a kindred gravity.

Even big Hank Lundermann seemed a trifle shocked by Blake's rash declaration. He asked, 'Just what was you figgerin' to do?'

'Raid the Skillet,' Blake said flatly.

Those three words brought another interval of silence. Then Jeb Hodnett muttered, 'That's a tol'able chore to handle, Dave. Strebor's bunch ain't gentle Annies, you know. They ain't men to be scared by words.'

The Spear H owner glanced deliberately around the ring of faces, as if searching for support. 'There's only seven of us, not counting Pike,' he pointed out.

Young Corvette said quickly, 'Count me in, and make it eight.'

Whereupon his father's face took on a deeper frown. 'I don't know about that, Pike. Your maw won't take kindly to havin' you galivant around as a gunrider. She won't cotton to it at all.'

Pike's boyish face flushed redly, that quick color making him look even more youthful. 'I'm no slickear,' he insisted. 'Come next Thursday I'll be twenty-one!'

'That's the way to talk,' Cliff Paddock praised, and then turned his attention to Dave Blake. 'What was your plan?' he inquired, as if anxious to keep this thing rolling toward a definite goal.

Blake said, 'Let's go where we can do some figgerin'.'

Beauregarde was the last to leave the bunkhouse. When he went outside, Blake was down on one knee, drawing a pattern in the dust with his finger. 'Here's the way it looks to me,' the Pool president explained. 'Strebor maintains line camps at the old Caliche place and at Spanish Butte. One is north and west of Skillet, the other southeast. If we was to take them two camps over and use 'em for a place to work from, we'd be able to hamstring the headquarters outfit in one week's time.'

'How about our own places?' Tate Corvette demanded. 'What's to keep the Skillet from raiding us, while we're down there?'

Dave Blake bristled visibly. 'Hell, man, there's no way of guarding against Skillet raids. Unless we knew ahead of time, we couldn't have enough men at a place to protect it. This way we'll keep Strebor's bunch so damn busy at Skillet they'll have no time for raids up here.'

'Mebbe yes, mebbe no,' Jeb Hodnett declared. 'Supposin' Strebor sends a raidin' party up here just the same?'

'That,' Blake announced, 'is the chance we'll have to take. I'm not saying my plan is foolproof. It'll mean plenty of riding and plenty of fighting, and some of us may not come back. But it's a chance to stop the Skillet, once and for all!'

Tate Corvette said moodily, 'Yeah—if we win.'

Young Oscar Ellison had remained silent thus far. Now he glanced at Beauregarde and asked, 'What do you think of the plan?'

It was a genuinely respectful question, yet Beauregarde sensed that the taint of his gunsmoke reputation was behind it. And besides, he wasn't a member of the Pool; merely a hired gunhawk. So he sent a questioning glance at Dave Blake before answering Oscar's question.

'Go ahead,' Blake said. 'I was going to ask you the same thing.'

Remembering what he'd learned the night before, Beauregarde took time to choose his words. He'd had no opportunity to tell Dave Blake about the consultation he'd witnessed at the Skillet. All lights had been out when he got home, and so far this morning there'd been no chance to talk privately with Blake. But the import of what he had seen and heard on the previous night held a definite bearing on this thing, and it influenced his speech now . . .

'It looks,' he said, 'like an even-up proposition to me. Strebor will be expecting trouble, but he won't know just when it's coming, nor from what direction.'

It occurred to him then that if there was a spy among these members of the Pool, Strebor *would* know, and knowing, would have all the best of it. But this suspicion seemed pretty flimsy, so Beauregarde temporarily discarded that angle from his thinking.

Hank Lundermann asked, 'You mean we'd stand as much chance of losing as we would of winning?'

'Yes,' Beauregarde muttered, 'but there's more to it than that. To my way of thinking, it depends on just how tough a bunch Strebor has on his payroll. If they can take punishment without dragging their picket pins, the Pool might not be strong enough to smash Skillet in one week, nor in two weeks. If Strebor is paying real high wages and his riders stick with him come hell or high water, then it'll be a long drawn out fight which could end only one way.'

'How's that?' Cliff Paddock demanded, his usually cheerful voice showing a quick displeasure at this pessimistic talk.

'Bankruptcy for your Pool, burned homes and fresh dug graves,' Beauregarde said quietly. 'That's how most range wars end.'

Dave Blake said irritably, 'Sure—sure. But I say it can be done in one week's time if we all hang and rattle together. Strebor's bunch ain't fighting for their homes. They'll run like rabbits if we dab it on 'em hard enough and fast enough!'

Beauregarde was on the point of admitting this possibility when Cliff Paddock exclaimed, 'Look—look who's coming!'

★   ★   ★

Susan Blake sat with Mrs. Corvette, Judy Lundermann and Della Ellison on the gallery. She was watching the men file out of the bunkhouse when Orphelia Corvette said bluntly, 'I don't like the idea of the Pool hiring a professional killer. It puts us in the same class with Sid Strebor, and it don't seem like a fitting thing for Christian folks to do!'

Susan smiled and, knowing how sharp a tongue this big woman had, remained silent.

But Della Ellison said quickly, 'I don't believe Mister Beauregarde is a professional killer. He's—he's just a man who knows how to use a gun when it's needed.'

Susan could well understand Della's defense of Beauregarde. Oscar's wife steadfastly contended that Beauregarde had killed Buck Casco solely to save her husband from certain death. But Susan was not prepared for Judy Lundermann's warm-voiced appraisal . . .

'I think Lee Beauregarde is the bravest man I've ever seen,' Judy declared. 'And also the best-looking.'

Mrs. Corvette's heavy cheeks tightened into a frown. 'Perhaps my son Pike will be interested to know how much you admire a Texas renegade,' she said acidly.

And Mrs. Hodnett murmured censuringly, 'You shouldn't make such fast decisions, Judy. You're too young to judge a man on such short acquaintance.'

Which was when Susan heard Cliff Paddock exclaim, 'Look—look who's coming!'

In that same instant, as she saw Sheriff Derbyshire ride into the yard with Sid Strebor and eight riders, amazement gripped Susan like a grasping hand. What could this mean?

94

Why had Sam Derbyshire come here with all these Skillet riders?

Then abruptly she guessed the answer, and guessing it, felt a cold finger of fear stab through her. Sheriff Sam's desire for peace at any price must have warped his reasoning; Derbyshire was taking this desperate means of blocking wide-open range war. And he was wrong—wrong as a man could be!

The gaunt lawman called, 'Howdy, Dave.'

He halted ten feet in front of the Pool group and dismounted. But Strebor didn't dismount. He sat stiffly alert, with his eight gunslingers fanned out behind him. Susan recognized the two trail tramps who'd been with Beauregarde that day on the flats; they flanked Strebor on either side. Just behind them was Ace-High Gregg, who had once owned a share in the Senate Saloon; Ben Smith who had killed a man in Tucson; and Dakota Dawson, an ex-gambler from Tombstone. The other three were recent arrivals at the Skillet . . .

They made a solid show of strength, those Skillet riders; gun-hung and hard-faced, they looked like wolves waiting for the kill. And so they were!

Susan heard her father ask gruffly, 'What's the idea of this, Sam? Why you stinking up my yard with that polecat bunch behind you?'

Sam Derbyshire said, 'Now take it easy, Dave. I'm here on official business . . .'

Susan didn't wait to hear the rest of it. She got up and, moving without haste, went into the house.

At sight of Derbyshire and Strebor, Lee Beauregarde remembered the conversation he'd overheard the night before—and guessed instantly why the men were there. For some unaccountable reason Sheriff Derbyshire had decided to arrest him for Casco's killing!

Yet even then, with that hunch hurtling through his mind, Beauregarde felt no animosity toward the old lawman. And when Derbyshire peered at him, saying, 'You're under arrest,' Beauregarde showed neither surprise nor resentment.

He inquired mildly, 'What's the charge?'

But before Derbyshire could answer, Dave Blake blurted, 'So you've sold out to Strebor! By God, I never thought you'd come to that Sam Derbyshire!'

This accusation jerked Derbyshire's attention away from Beauregarde. His angular face flushed darkly, and for one tense instant he seemed on the verge of rushing headlong at Dave Blake. Then he said, 'There ain't another goddam man in this valley could say that without backin' it with his fists.'

'I'll back it,' Dave Blake declared brashly. 'I'll back it any way you like!'

It was a thing to see, a thing to remember; Those two oldsters standing stiffly face to face like two mossyhorned old bulls bellowing out their fighting spirit. But because one of them reminded Lee Beauregarde of his dead father, and the other had saved his life, he stepped quickly between them.

'What,' he asked Derbyshire, 'is the charge against me?'

'Brand blotting,' the sheriff said.

For a fleeting instant Beauregarde's mind failed to function. He peered at Derbyshire, and asked wonderingly, 'Brand blotting?'

The lawman nodded. A badgered expression crept into his deep-socketed eyes, and he said, 'You're charged with changin' a Skillet into an O Bar E on a grulla steer.'

All the puzzlement ran out of Beauregarde in one wave of utter astonishment. So that was the kind of bargain Derbyshire had made with Sid Strebor last night!

'You're loco as a goddam hoot owl!' Dave Blake shouted. 'Why would Beauregarde blot a brand for Oscar Ellison?'

Sid Strebor said slyly, 'Beauregarde killed a man for Ellison, didn't he?'

That sharp lance of words set Blake back on his heels. And it struck each member of the Pool with the same startling impact. Looking beyond Derbyshire, Beauregarde saw satisfaction put a brighter glint in Strebor's inky eyes. There was something queerly repulsive about this small-bodied man; something that put a crawling itch into Beauregarde's right hand. Here, he thought angrily, was a man built in the image of a human being yet who was utterly devoid of human decency. Strebor had the merciless instincts of a crafty killer wolf, and he was proving those instincts now. Using the impending conflict as a lever, he had badgered Derbyshire into this crazy deal with a promise of peaceful settlement—a promise that would be broken to bloody fragments the moment it had served its purpose.

Stomping down the urge that tempted him to draw and shoot Sid Strebor as he'd shoot a snake, Beauregarde switched his gaze to Derbyshire and asked, 'Why bring all the company with you, sheriff? Don't you like to ride alone?'

Derbyshire sent a roving glance around the Pool members and then spoke directly to Dave Blake. 'I asked Strebor to come here for a confab to see if there wasn't some way we could settle the trouble peaceable. First off he refused. Said I didn't arrest Beauregarde like I should've, and make him stand trial for Casco's killing. Sid claims that Beauregarde did the brand blotting for Ellison, and that if I'll arrest Beauregarde on that charge he'll talk things over with your Pool.'

Dave Blake heard him out in frowning silence. Then he said quietly, almost whisperingly, 'You know goddam well Beauregarde didn't blot the brand, so why you runnin' off at the mouth this way?'

'No,' Derbyshire contradicted. 'I don't *know* it. It's my guess he didn't. But that's no reason why I should refuse to arrest him when a charge is brought against him. My opinion ain't enough, Dave, and neither is yours. It's up to a jury to decide if he's guilty or innocent.'

The sheriff shifted his gaze to the women and youngsters on the gallery. 'I hate to see this country busted wide open by range war when it ain't necessary. Strebor says he's willing to settle things peaceable and legal if you folks will do the same.'

'What's arresting Beauregarde got to do with it?' Hank Lundermann demanded.

And Dave Blake snapped, 'Just a way of hamstringing the Pool. Strebor wants all the gunhawks on his side!'

Which was, Beauregarde reflected, as near to truth as anything that had been said so far. Sid Strebor knew no jury would convict him. Hell, the chances were a hundred to one that Strebor didn't even intend to have him reach jail. Glancing over to Faro Savoy's saddle-slumped frame, Beauregarde saw the malevolent gleam in the reedy rider's eyes and guessed Savoy suspected who had hit him the night before. Faro would most likely be glad to act as executioner of a prisoner . . .

'Let's hear the rest of Sam's proposition,' Tate Corvette suggested.

The little cowman, Beauregarde decided, was a thorough pacifist—made so by long association with a woman who outweighed him a hundred pounds or more.

Oscar Ellison opened his mouth to speak, but Dave Blake growled quickly, 'We ain't listening to no proposition based on Beauregarde's arrest. That's final as she stands!'

'Is the Pool a one-man outfit?' Sid Strebor inquired caustically.

Red Valentine chuckled, and sounds of amusement reverberated rapidly through the Skillet group in taunting echo. It was as if those riders knew this whole deal was a farce, and were enjoying it immensely.

Yet here, at this very moment, was the beginning of wholesale tragedy. Here was the making of dissension that would destroy the Pool's unity and bring disaster. Recognizing it, and foreseeing the outcome, Beauregarde's lips eased into a mirthless smile. It was ironic that his presence here should be the final straw which broke the Pool's last strand of unity . . .

Derbyshire spoke again, patiently, with urgent appeal riding his voice. 'First off I take Beauregarde in,' he said. 'Then tomorrow we hold a meeting at the Acme Hotel and figger out a deal that will be satisfactory to both sides. What do you say to that?'

'No,' Dave Blake shouted. 'Not by a damned sight!'

Derbyshire ignored him. He looked to Tate Corvette and asked, 'As a member of the Panamint Pool, what's your vote?'

Corvette rubbed his palms together, glanced at Jeb Hodnett, at Lundermann, and finally at Blake. 'I think we should talk it over,' he said finally. 'I vote yes.'

Quickly then Derbyshire looked to Hodnett. 'How about you, Jeb?'

Hodnett nodded. 'If there's any way to avoid a fight, I'm for it,' he declared.

Hank Lundermann was next, and he drawled, 'Hell, I don't see no harm in holdin' a meetin' in town. It'll give us a chance to sample Honest John's whiskey.'

Derbyshire, plainly pleased with the way things were going, said, 'That's three out of six, Dave. Guess that shows the way the wind is blowing.'

'Yes,' Blake said sourly, 'it does. It shows you've busted up the Pool, good and proper. But, by God, you ain't going to while he's on my property!'

That challenge wiped the grin from Derbyshire's face. He said quickly, 'The Pool ain't busted, Dave, and there's no call for you to git proddy. I came here to arrest Beauregarde, and he ain't offered no objections.'

Abruptly then all eyes turned to Beauregarde, and Cliff Paddock asked eagerly, 'What's your idea, smokeroo?'

For a brief moment Beauregarde considered the advisability of ending this deadlock by surrendering to Derbyshire. But almost at once he remembered his hunch that Strebor had no intention of letting him reach Apache Tank alive. It would be an easy thing for Faro Savoy or Red Valentine to cut him down on the pretext he'd attempted to escape . . .

So he said quietly, 'No, I guess not. Never did like jails,' and saw surprise change to disappointment in Sam Derbyshire's old eyes.

'Don't make things no worse than they are,' the sheriff pleaded. 'You'll git a fair trial.'

Dave Blake moved in beside Beauregarde, and Cliff Paddock closed the gap on the other side. This shift left Oscar Ellison standing with young Pike Corvette and the other three members of the Pool. Ellison glanced questioningly at Sheriff Derbyshire, then walked over and stood beside Paddock. Whereupon Dave Blake smiled and motioned at the lawman. 'You ain't arresting nobody here today,' he declared brashly. 'Git off my land and take your polecat bunch with you!'

Beauregarde guessed at once that Derbyshire wouldn't obey that order. And remembering the things that had made his own father a good lawman, he understood the paradoxical qualities which would cause this peace-loving sheriff to fight for a prisoner.

Jeb Hodnett said worriedly, 'Wait, Dave. Let's talk this over.'

But Sid Strebor spoiled that plea for tolerance by saying, 'Well, Derbyshire—how about some law and order?'

Derbyshire peered bleakly at Beauregarde. 'Surrender—or take the consequences,' he ordered.

And in that same instant, as Red Valentine and Faro Savoy moved up behind the sheriff with guns already drawn, Orphelia Corvette called shrilly, 'Pike—you come away from there!'

CHAPTER FOUR

For upwards of fifteen minutes Susan Blake had stood beside the open kitchen window with her father's heavy .45-.90 rifle in her hands. She had prayed there'd be no need to use it, and remembering that she had never fired this big gun, hoped fervently she wouldn't have to fire it.

Yet, because she had a thorough knowledge of her father's rash pride, she had realized at once that there might be but one way to prevent a shoot-out between him and Sam Derbyshire. For though Sheriff Sam was a patient and peaceful man, he also had his pride.

Derbyshire was standing a little past the window; Strebor and his men had halted directly opposite. They were less than twenty feet away, and thus it was that Susan glimpsed the signal which the Skillet's boss gave the two riders beside him—saw them stealthily draw their guns and move forward.

Whereupon she lifted the heavy rifle, thumbed back the hammer and, aiming the weapon directly at Sid Strebor, called 'Sheath those guns—or I'll shoot!'

In that instant Susan's sense clicked to an amazing clarity of perception. All those sunlit men were suddenly etched into sharper focus; their movements were so slow and deliberate that the turning of their heads seemed to take a full moment. She saw surprise widen Sid Strebor's eyes; heard a gusty grunt slide from the lips of the blocky-faced rider behind Derbyshire and saw two scarlet spots flame in the other gunhawk's chalky cheeks.

For a queerly suspended interval no one moved nor spoke nor seemed to breathe. The yard's sudden stillness was like the hush of death. The pounding of her pulse was loud in her ears; suspense built up until it became an intolerable pressure against her wire-taut nerves, and in that timeless interval she was aware of a desolate isolation—of being utterly alone.

It was a strangely terrifying sensation; a monstrous, overwhelming sensation. Nothing seemed real nor sensible nor familiar. Those yonderly faces were the grotesque masks of men she'd never seen. Even the yard seemed different, somehow; its dust sparkled in the sunshine, but it was cold, like snow, or ice. And the room seemed different, as if she'd never been there before.

Then abruptly she glimpsed the blurring motion of Lee Beauregarde's right arm, and heard his voice shatter that outside stillness with an order: 'Leather your guns!' Then she saw the two Skillet riders slowly sheathe their weapons.

The rest of it was like the swift opening of a familiar door. All the cold sense of unreality vanished, and she no longer felt alone. She watched Cliff Paddock and her father draw their guns; she saw the stiff way Oscar Ellison stood, empty-handed—saw Jeb Hodnett, Hank Lundermann, Tate Corvette and young Pike standing as if stunned beyond the power of movement. And she heard Orphelia Corvette call insistently, 'Pike—come away from there this instant!'

Susan lowered the heavy rifle. Abruptly then

her hands began to tremble, their sudden shaking so violent that she dared not uncock the hammer. Leaning the gun against the wall, she dropped weakly into a chair, and heard her father order gruffly, 'Now git—quick!'

For a moment, while quivering weakness had its way with her, those outside voices merged into a meaningless jumble of hurried conversation. Then there was a drumming thud of hoofs, that sound swiftly diminishing; and the smell of risen dust. The thought came to her that even though she might not have marshalled enough courage to shoot Sid Strebor, her threat had given Lee Beauregarde a chance to draw his gun . . .

And hard on the heels of that thought came another—the startling realization that it had been Lee Beauregarde who had snatched her from that awful void of aloneness. Not Cliff Paddock; not her father. But Beauregarde, whom she'd once spurned as 'your kind of killer!'

She was thinking about that, and taking a queer pride in the peculiar pardnership they'd just shared, when Judy Lundermann rushed into the kitchen and exclaimed, 'You did it, Susan! You turned the tables on that Skillet bunch!'

Susan smiled. She picked up the .45-.90 and carefully lowered the hammer. Her hands were steady now; they were strong and capable, like

Lee Beauregarde's brown hands . . .

Judy said enviously, 'I never thought you had it in you, Susan Blake. I didn't know you had nerve enough to shoot a man!'

Whereupon Susan smiled again. 'I don't know either,' she admitted frankly, glancing out at Lee Beauregarde's high shape as he sauntered toward the wagonshed. 'I'm glad I didn't have to find out.'

★   ★   ★

Hank Lundermann was the last Pool member to make his preparations for departure. He took a long time to tighten his saddle cinch; he kept glancing at Blake and Paddock, who sat hunkered on their heels in front of the gallery steps. A low plume of dust trailed Tate Corvette's wagon down the road, and off to the south Jeb Hodnett's horse was loping steadily homeward.

Judy Lundermann was already in saddle. She eased her pony over to the wagonshed, where Beauregarde had resumed his repair work on the ripped scabbard. She said, 'They're gray, aren't they, Texican?'

Beauregarde glanced up at her and, seeing the open admiration in her brown eyes, felt a sudden embarrassment. 'Reckon so,' he drawled.

This shapely daughter of Hank Lundermann

had an almost brazen way of meeting a man's glances. It was as if she welcomed his appraisal, wanted him to join her in mutual admiration. She had grown up with only men and boys around her, and that rough environment had strongly marked her manners; but it hadn't spoiled the seductive quality of her heavy lidded eyes nor the softness of her red lips.

Hank Lundermann climbed into the saddle and, glancing her way, said, 'Come on Judy.'

Then he turned to Blake and said, 'I'll think it over, Dave. I'll let you know in a day or so.'

'Don't want your help,' Blake replied, a gruff intolerance in his voice. 'The Panamint Pool is busted, and I'm some particular who sides Three Links against the Skillet. Quite some particular.'

That rebuke brought a blotched redness to Lundermann's beefy face. 'What the hell you expect a man to do?' he demanded.

'I expect a man to be a man,' Blake declared, 'not a belly-crawlin' coward.'

He got up and, turning his back to Lundermann, joined Susan, Della and Oscar on the gallery.

Lundermann called sharply, 'Judy—come on!'

She said, for Beauregarde's ears alone, 'I'll talk him into siding Dave. Stop by and see us, Texican.'

Then she rode on out of the yard with her father.

Cliff Paddock joined the group on the gallery, and presently Blake called, 'Come on over, Lee.'

That use of his first name pleased Beauregarde. It made him feel less like a gunsmoke pariah. And when he reached the steps Susan said, 'I'm in Oscar's class now. Your quick draw got me out of a bad situation.'

Paddock patted Susan's shoulder affectionately. 'That big muzzle of the .45-.90 you pointed at Strebor got us all out of a hole,' he announced. 'Those two old chums of Beauregarde's had us dead to rights.'

The Boxed P owner was grinning when he said it, but Beauregarde sensed a strand of jealousy in Paddock's voice. And he felt a rousing resentment against this man's loose use of the words 'smokeroo' and 'chums.'

He said, 'I rode into this country with Valentine and Savoy, but they never were my chums. I'd like you to get that straight—and remember it.'

'All right—all right,' Paddock agreed good-naturedly. 'What I meant was that Susan's bluff got us out of a tight.'

'Mebbe,' Beauregarde suggested, 'she wasn't bluffing.'

Della Ellison put in warmly, 'It was a brave

thing for her to do. I'd never had been able to do it.'

'Looks like there'll be a chance for plenty of brave stunts around here soon,' Dave Blake prophesied. There was a prideful look in his eyes as he glanced at Susan, but it didn't get into his voice when he said, 'How about a bite of food, Susie?'

The two girls went into the house then, and Cliff Paddock asked, 'What now, Dave? How do we handle it from here on?'

'We can't tackle the Skillet,' Blake reflected, 'Not just the four of us. Reckon I'll have to sell some beef and hire me a crew of gunriders. Either that, or throw in my cards.'

'You think the Skillet will tackle us?' Ellison inquired.

Blake made a shrugging motion with his shoulders and said, 'What else would you expect a greedy hog like Strebor to do?'

Covertly watching the old boss of Three Links, Beauregarde saw an expression in Blake's eyes that hadn't been there before. Beneath their shaggy brows those eyes were bleak as barren rooms. The old fire was gone from them, departed with his high hope of smashing the Skillet in one week's time. The breakup of the Pool had been a hard blow to this old warrior; a tremendous blow. It had disrupted all Blake's plans; had hamstrung his hell-for-leather scheme of striking in the swift and only way that would bring quick victory. Now that scheme was gone—and his rash confidence had gone with it.

Oscar Ellison began pacing nervously along the gallery.

Cliff Paddock put his fingers to shaping up a smoke; and when he offered the tobacco sack to Blake, Beauregarde noticed the cameo ring again. It was, he thought, a peculiar sort of ring for a cowman to be wearing. It seemed out of place on so rugged a hand . . .

Paddock lit his cigarette and said thoughtfully, 'Wonder what Strebor's next move will be.'

And at that same moment Oscar Ellison exclaimed, 'Smoke off there to the south!'

They all moved to the gallery's end, and saw the blackish plume boiling up over the distant hills.

'There's the answer,' Dave Blake said bitterly. 'That's your shack, Cliff.'

'Yeah,' Paddock muttered. 'It sure as hell is.'

★　　★　　★

For the next three days comparative quiet reigned in Panamint Valley. And during that period of false peace, four men rode from dawn till dark, chousing Three Link steers out of the brush. Then, as they were saddling up on the morning of the fourth day, Hank Lundermann and Pike Corvette rode into the yard and declared their intention of 'giving a hand.'

'Judy won't give me no rest,' Lundermann explained. 'She hid my likker and threatened to move into town if I didn't come over here. She says you're right, and I got the same notion.'

'Me too,' Pike Corvette declared. 'I'm twenty-one now—my own boss!'

Hearing this, and guessing what it meant to Dave Blake, Beauregarde watched the old man closely. For a moment the frowning arrogance remained on Blake's sun-blackened face; then his eyes crinkled at the corners and he was smiling for the first time since the Pool had broken up . . .

'You're welcome as summer rain,' he declared, and nodded toward the milling saddle band in the corral. 'Rope yourselves fresh hosses and we'll get a wiggle on ourselves.'

That day's beef gather doubled the small herd held in Box Canyon, and when Blake led his five-man crew home to supper he said cheerfully, 'Couple more days will do it. We'll start our drive to town right after supper Thursday night. Traveling cool, the steers won't lose much tallow, and if Joe Fagan has a buyer I'll have me a gunhawk crew all hired by this time next week!'

Judy Lundermann stood on the gallery with Susan and Della Ellison. Seeing her there, Beauregarde knew why Pike Corvette had chosen to assert his manly rights. Judy was a girl to make a man remember campfire dreams, and seeing the way Pike kept glancing toward the house as he unsaddled, Beauregarde smiled thinly. Oscar Ellison was already hurrying across the yard to Della, and Paddock had called a greeting to Susan. These three had someone waiting for them when the day's grueling toil was over. And they had something to look forward to when the war should be over—something a vengeance-prodded trail tramp would never have.

After supper lots were drawn to see who would stand guard out at Box Canyon. Paddock drew the first shift to midnight, and Beauregarde drew the late guard. He said good night and sauntered to the bunkhouse for some early sleep. But though he was dog tired, he was still awake when Paddock and Susan saddled up and rode off toward Box Canyon. Paddock, he reflected, had all the luck. He wondered if Susan would have offered to accompany him if he'd drawn first guard. And because he knew she wouldn't have, Beauregarde felt a growing animosity toward Cliff Paddock.

Some time later he heard Pike and Judy talking quietly over by the windmill, and some time after that he went to sleep.

When he awoke he contemplated the position of the night's crescent moon and decided it was close to midnight. The combined snoring of two men in nearby bunks told him that Lundermann and Pike had turned in; when he stepped out into the yard he saw that the house was dark—and wondered if Susan was still out at Box Canyon with Paddock.

The hunch that she was nagged at his mind all the way to the canyon. He endeavored to ignore it, to tell himself that she was scheduled to marry Paddock and, even if she weren't, he'd have no right to court her. Hell, he was just a back-trail drifter with a debt to pay. Even though Susan had shown him an increasing friendliness these past few days, he had no cause to place too much importance on her smiles, nor on the more intimate tone of her voice. Susan Blake was a proud and proper girl being nice to her father's only hired hand.

So thinking, he rode into the holding ground and found Cliff Paddock standing guard alone. Whereupon all his animosity toward the man vanished and he said cheerfully, 'It's a real fine night for riding.'

'Yeah,' Paddock agreed yawningly, 'and fine for sleeping also.'

He rode off then, and later, when Beauregarde rimmed the circular wall of the canyon, he thought he heard a horse running off somewhere south of Three Links. But it was only a remote rumor and it soon faded . . .

★   ★   ★

At noon on Thursday, while they were eating saddle-pocket lunches, Dave Blake said, 'We've got us a beef herd. When we chouse this bunch into the canyon, we'll have upwards of three hundred head.'

'Too bad you got to sell 'em this early,' Hank Lundermann mused. 'They'd bring a lot more money in the fall.'

Blake said stubbornly, 'I need a strong fighting crew right now. Next fall would be too late.'

Then he turned to Beauregarde. 'Reckon we can finish up without you, Lee. Take a pasear down toward Skyline ridge and see if Skillet has been scouting our range. I got a peculiar feeling in my gizzard. Things been too peaceable these last few days.'

That same thought had been in Beauregarde's mind. Nothing tangible, nor definite; just an obscure premonition that this roundup was progressing too smoothly.

Cliff Paddock said, 'I had the same hunch the other night, Dave. Took a circle south before I turned in. But I didn't see a thing.'

'Strebor is waiting for you to bring the fight

to him,' Lundermann prophesied. 'He ain't in no hurry. Not now, with the Pool all split up.'

Which was, Beauregarde decided, a reasonable opinion. Yet, because he'd once been suspicious of Lundermann, he recognized the possibility that the Lazy L owner might be talking one way and thinking another. If Strebor knew about this beef drive tonight, he could wreck Blake's desperate play to hire a fighting crew . . .

Beauregarde was thinking about that as he rode southward and came face to face with Susan on a timbered ridge just north of Three Links.

She said pleasantly, 'Rode up to find out what time you brush poppers would be in for supper. Dad said he hoped to finish early.'

'He will,' Beauregarde informed her, feeling the high flare of interest this girl's presence always gave him. 'Two-three hours will see it finished, which means we'll get a daylight start for Apache Tank.'

'Then I'd better go back and arrange an early supper,' Susan decided, and fell in beside him. 'Where you heading for?'

'Just fiddling around,' he said, and because the nagging premonition of trouble was still with him, he asked, 'How well do you know Hank Lundermann?'

That question seemed to surprise her. She

said, 'Why, real well, I guess. What makes you ask?'

Beauregarde had intended to request her opinion on the possibility of Lundermann being a spy for Skillet. But now he evaded the issue. Having a hunch about a man was one thing; putting it into words was another. 'I was just wondering about him,' he said lamely.

Susan gave him a contemplative regard, her eyes frankly searching as they'd been that first day they'd met. 'Were you wondering about Lundermann—or about his daughter?' she asked finally, a taunting note in her voice.

Her question surprised Beauregarde. It showed him how her thoughts were shaping; how deep and direct her perceptions were. She had seen Judy speak to him only that one time in the dooryard, but she was guessing now that there'd been other meetings. And knowing Judy's impetuous ways, she was wondering about them . . .

'Judy,' she said, 'thinks you're a sort of White Knight in shining armor.'

Beauregarde grinned. 'Guess there's no danger of you mistaking me for a White Knight, is there, ma'am?'

'No,' she said slowly. 'No, not the slightest danger.'

Some secret thought curved her lips in a faint, ironic smile, and she added, 'You aren't what I supposed you to be at first. I'm not

117

sure just what you are, but I know one thing. You've seen too much and you've hated too much. It's made you older and tougher than you should be.'

That brought a self-mocking grin to Beauregarde's long lips; caused him to use the same words she had once used at a similar point in a previous conversation: 'My—what sharp eyes you have.'

They both laughed at that, and for a time they rode in reflective silence across the high-arched back of the wooded hill. The air there was crisp, rarefied; it held the fragrance of sun-warmed pine needles, of dried grama grass and late-flowering wolf tail. Hazy shafts of sunlight slanting through parade-like stands of lodgepole pine gave the place a sequestered, cathedral-like atmosphere and made it a fitting place for reflection.

Save for the muffled tromp of their horses, no sound disturbed the day's siesta silence, and during this interval of slow riding, Lee Beauregarde basked in a strange warm sense of well-being. This, he reflected, was the way life should be. A man wasn't made to ride alone. And he wasn't meant to ride in constant vigilance; to be forever probing the shadows of the trail, always on guard against the nefarious designs of his fellowmen. There should be times when a man could relax in the presence of his chosen companion; times like this, when one woman's cherished sweetness merged with the clean, sweet-scented aroma of nature's high places.

It occurred to him abruptly that he'd never had such thoughts before—that until that very moment he hadn't realized how utterly alone he'd been. Oh, there'd been the dismal sense of lack and loneliness; of always being a stranger. But this was different, more basic and more fundamental. It was a sharp awareness of how much a man could miss in life. And with that recognition came a profound conviction that this girl beside him—this blonde girl with warm blue eyes and curving lips—had the power to make him sense the dregs of futility or lift him to high pinnacles of exaltation . . .

As if there were some magic strand of soundless communication between them, Susan asked softly, 'Don't you ever get tired of living like a renegade?'

Her face was turned directly toward him. In the alternating shafts of sunlight and shadow it was revealed in changing tints of soft ivory, of old rose and living gold that gave it an exotic loveliness. For a full moment he looked at her as a man looks at some rare and priceless gem. Then a whimsical smile quirked his lips and he drawled, 'Yes—but that doesn't change it. I'm still a renegade.'

'But you're not,' she insisted, emphasizing

that declaration by resting her hand on his arm.

It was, he saw, a slender, supple hand. Her left one. And it was unadorned. Abruptly then he recognized a fact which he had thus far failed to notice—she wasn't wearing an engagement ring!

The significance of that discovery made him recall the question she'd been on the point of answering that night by the horse corral. Releasing the knotted reins, Beauregarde reached up and covered those slim fingers in a gesture no more than comradely, yet which built a higher and higher excitement in him.

'You never did tell me when the ceremony was going to be,' he suggested.

She withdrew her fingers and said smilingly, 'I thought women were the curious ones.' Then she added, 'The wedding won't be until Cliff does one very important thing.'

'Secret?'

'No, although very few people know it. Everyone seems to take it for granted that we're to be married soon. Even Dad.'

'Aren't you?' he asked, wholly puzzled.

She shook her head. 'Not unless Cliff succeeds much faster than he has so far.'

They had reached the east rim of the hill now, and Three Links sprawled below them. Beauregarde asked, 'Mind telling me what the important thing is that Paddock has to do?'

Susan halted, and when she glanced up at him there was an impish twinkle in her eyes. 'Cliff,' she murmured, 'has to convince me that I really love him. Up to now he hasn't done it.'

That unexpected announcement jolted Lee Beauregarde completely. It brought a buoyancy that lifted him to high-riding gladness. He asked, 'Then you haven't promised to marry Paddock?'

'No,' she said. 'There's been no promise, Lee.'

Her voice was warm, intimate. And she was close, as she'd been that other time when the impulse to take her in his arms had been too strong to resist. And so it was now. The desire to kiss those gently smiling lips was like a rising flame inside him. Yet, because self-discipline was part and parcel of the creed he lived by, Beauregarde held himself in check a moment longer.

'Mebbe you'd better go,' he suggested.

But she didn't go—and her lips were entirely smiling when he kissed them.

For a pulsing, timeless interval, Beauregarde forgot all his back-trail ghosts. He forgot everything but this girl who held herself rigidly in his arms for a moment and then, relaxing, returned his kiss. The flavor of her lips was like some rare and intoxicating wine.

It roused all his hungers, fanned embers of emotion long dormant and neglected. His arms drew her closer and closer, until the beating of her heart was a tangible throb against his chest—until presently her hands pressed for release and she said breathlessly, 'Please, Lee!'

Whereupon Beauregarde grudgingly let her go, and watched her fingers dart to their instinctive task of rearranging her tumbled hair. He had thought it was a thoroughly feminine gesture the first time he'd witnessed it. But now, with the flavor of her kiss still on his lips, he decided it was the most pleasing gesture he had ever seen . . .

He said gustily, 'I wish you'd answered my question about the ceremony a week ago, Susan.'

'The answer wouldn't have been quite the same then,' she murmured, sudden embarrassment giving her oval face a peach-bloom loveliness. 'That was before you rescued me—the day I aimed Dad's rifle at Sid Strebor.'

Beauregarde was considering that and not quite understanding it, when she added, 'A week ago I thought you were a renegade.'

'And now?' he prompted, still puzzled.

'Now I know you're not. Well, at least you aren't just a shiftless drifter trying to make a living with a gun. What started you on the trail, Lee? A girl?'

He shook his head. He had never seen fit to divulge the reason for his nomadic existence. But it seemed right and fitting that he should tell this girl, and so he told her.

'Three years,' she mused. 'And you're still looking?'

'Yeah—that's why I came here. Intended to look around and keep going. But my plans got sidetracked.'

'And when this trouble here is over, you'll go on—until you find Roberts?'

'Or die of old age,' he muttered. 'Revenge isn't a pleasant thing to live for, and I won't exactly enjoy killing Roberts. But I'll never feel right until I do.'

She reached out and touched his arm again, and said, 'I'm sorry for misjudging you, Lee. I—I saw the hard look in your eyes, and the way you wore your gun in a tied-down holster. Well, you *look* like a renegade, even though you're not.'

'Gunsmoke has a way of marking a man,' Beauregarde said. 'One shooting scrape leads to another, and after a while he's just a spooky galoot with the stink of gunsmoke in his hair.'

He put his fingers to building a cigarette and said wonderingly, 'Were you bluffing, that day you pointed the rifle at Sid Strebor?'

'I don't know, Lee. Honestly I don't. But

I'm glad you saved me from finding out.'

'My Dad once warned me never to draw a gun unless I was prepared to use it,' he said. 'I'm passing that same advice on to you, Susan. Don't ever point a gun at a man unless you're willing to pull the trigger—and pull it before he does. A bluff like that might cost you your life sometime.'

'I'll remember,' she promised.

Then she exclaimed, 'I forgot all about getting an early supper! I've got work to do, Gallant Knight!' And putting spurs to her horse, she rode down the slope at a run.

Beauregarde watched her until she became a small and resolute shape drifting above the buckbrush. Then he rode southward, feeling more cheerful than he'd felt in many a month . . .

★   ★   ★

A watcher, stationed on the crest of Skyline Ridge and viewing Skillet's yard through powerful field-glasses, would have witnessed unmistakable activity that Thursday afternoon. With his glasses focused properly, he would have noted the whiskey keg on the bunkhouse stoop and the riders grouped around it like flies swarming around a sugar bowl.

Had the watcher been familiar with the

faces of the Skillet's riding crew, he would have recognized Faro Savoy, whose chalky cheeks and feverish eyes flamed with the killer courage whiskey always gave him; Ben Smith, whose hamlike hands were fondly forcing an oily rag through the barrel of a Spencer rifle; Dakota Dawson with the sightless snouts of matched .44s protruding below his tied-down half-breed holsters.

The watcher would have also recognized Ace-High Gregg, Bat Folliard, Pete Crow and Baldy Severide. But he wouldn't have been able to name the four new riders who completed the bunkhouse group. For these four hard-faced hombres had arrived at the Skillet yesterday, freshly imported from Tombstone—bounty killers beckoned by the beacon of high pay.

Shifting his field-glasses slightly, the watcher could have glimpsed the line of saddled horses standing in hipshot patience at the long kak pole near the corral gate. Counting them, he would have tallied thirteen horses. An unlucky number, according to superstition; a strong number, though, if gunslick riders filled those saddles. Thirteen horses—thirteen guns.

With another slight shift of direction the watcher could have sighted swarthy, fox-faced Sid Strebor standing in the shaded doorway of the ranch house with Red

Valentine. And even though he couldn't have heard their conversation, the watcher might have guessed the ominous portent of the things he saw—might have grasped their full significance. But there was no watcher with field-glasses on Skyline Ridge that day . . .

And although Lee Beauregarde rode a thorough, searching course across the range from Horseshoe Mesa to Gooseneck Divide, he found no fresh sign of horseback travel—save the tracks of the night scouting trip Cliff Paddock had mentioned to Dave Blake that afternoon. The Skillet hadn't scouted Three Links range. That much was certain.

Satisfied on this score, and still basking in the high glow of Susan's surrendering embrace, Beauregarde turned his bronc into the wheel-rutted roadway atop the divide. There he halted, giving his horse a brief breathing spell. This, he remembered, was the same spot where he'd viewed Three Links for the first time. Recalling the details of that occasion, he smiled reflectively. Susan hadn't been overly cordial that night; she had treated him with cool reserve, in the manner of a proud girl conversing with a six-gun smokeroo.

A lot had happened · since that night. Surprising, unexpected things. Violence, and the threat of violence, had brought many changes. There'd been the brand blotching of a Skillet steer, the burning of Oscar Ellison's house and of Paddock's shack, the breakup of the Pool, and Sam Derbyshire's frantic attempt for compromise. But the greatest change, and the most surprising, had been in himself. He had arrived in Panamint Valley a bitter, hate-prodded gunwolf with one grim purpose—revenge. There'd been no thought of romance in him, nor hint of any emotion except hate. Now all that was changed, and although his hatred for the murderer of his father was still a festering, unhealed sore inside him, it wasn't his chief emotion. It didn't dominate his thinking, nor motivate his every action as it had before he'd met Susan Blake. The need for vengeance was a real and urgent need, but he was no longer a man living by hate alone.

Gazing out across the sun-hammered hills and meadows that made up the southern portion of Three Links range, Beauregarde gave it a lingering regard. His premonition of impending trouble, he guessed, had been premature. Perhaps the peace of the past few days wasn't just a lull preceding a storm. No Skillet rider could have come close enough to glimpse the beef roundup without leaving sign somewhere along this strip of range.

And there was no sign . . .

Yet, at that very moment, as Beauregarde headed his horse homeward, Sid Strebor stood in the doorway at the Skillet, giving final instructions to Red Valentine—instructions that would rip the lid of false peace from Panamint Valley and turn it into a bloody holocaust of death and destruction.

'I don't want no mistakes made tonight,' Strebor announced. 'This is the best chance I'll ever have to put Dave Blake out of business. It's the chance I've been waiting on for two years. I'll handle the trail herd end of tonight's party with ten men, which should be enough to turn the whole damn outfit into buzzard bait. You and Savoy hold off on your stuff at Three Links until the herd gets through Big Sandy Wash. I don't want Blake turning back before we hit him. I want him and his beef steers and his riders all lined up for my surprise party.'

Red Valentine's flat lips stretched into a confident grin. 'It's goin' to be a busy night,' he reflected with plain relish. 'Visiting Three Links will be a pleasure, for a fact. I been wanting to get another look at Blake's fancy-faced daughter—a real close look.'

'Do all the damn looking you want,' Strebor muttered. 'You'll have plenty of time. When you get through with your social chores, put them three females into a rig and turn 'em loose. But be damned sure there's nothing left to look at when you leave Three Links. I want everything smashed—the windmill and corrals and bunkhouse. Everything!'

Strebor lifted a black cigar from his shirt pocket, bit off its end and spat it out. 'By God, I want Blake's place blasted so goddam high the pieces won't even fall back into the yard!'

Valentine nodded understandingly. He kept glancing at the whiskey keg over on the bunkhouse stoop. But Strebor wasn't finished with his instructions. He said, 'Don't let your female funnin' interfere with your work over there tonight. You'll have lots of time for both, because there won't be a Three Links rider loose when we get through with that trail herd.'

'How about Derbyshire?' Valentine inquired. 'What's he goin' to say about our big party?'

Cigar smoke spiraled lazily from Strebor's puckered lips. He was, at that moment, the living image of absolute confidence. Self-satisfaction was written on his smiling face; it glinted in his black eyes and dribbled from his smirking lips. 'I don't give a goddam what Derbyshire says—or what he thinks,' Strebor declared. 'Derbyshire is just a fussy old woman with a tin-star on his vest. He can't do a thing—not a goddam thing. Three Links was branded an outlaw spread the day Blake ran

Derbyshire off without arresting Beauregarde. Blake threatened a peace officer who wanted to arrest a brand-blotcher. Hodnett and Corvette were witnesses to that, and after we get through tonight we'll have no trouble with them two gentle Annies. They'll do what I tell 'em, and so will everybody else in this Valley. If Derbyshire don't line up with me, I'll get my own sheriff elected. How'd you like to wear a badge, Red—a nice, new shiny badge with sheriff printed on it?'

'That'd pleasure me considerable,' Valentine chuckled. 'It would for a fact. I always did cotton to town livin'. There's two-three Mex gals in Apache Tank I'd like time to investigate.'

'By God, you got wimmin on the brain!' Strebor accused impatiently. 'Don't you never think of nothing else?'

'Sure,' Valentine said. 'Sure I do. I'm thinkin' right now about that keg of whiskey over there. And about bein' sheriff. A lawdog job would suit me fine.'

Strebor said thoughtfully. 'You may get to wear a star at that, Red. Real soon. All it'll take is an election, with Skillet riders doing most of the voting. It could be held by this time next week—a special election. And within one day's time I'd have this whole valley under control. I knew it could be done the first day I rode into Apache Tank. I knew all it needed

130

was brains and the right kind of equipment. I got both, Red.'

'Yeah,' Valentine agreed, and glanced at the box of dynamite just inside the doorway. 'You sure as hell have.'

Strebor motioned toward the bunkhouse group. 'They've got enough likker to put 'em in the proper mood for fighting. Take that keg away and see that they've got extra shells for their saddle guns. They're going to get plenty of practice with their shooting between now and sunup tomorrow morning. Plenty practice!'

CHAPTER FIVE

Sunset was painting the high hills in harlequin hues when the Three Links trail herd left Box Canyon. 'We'll take it slow and easy,' Dave Blake announced. 'I ain't exactly expecting trouble, but I don't want this beef all bunched up for butchering in case something happens. Keep 'em strung out.'

He and Hank Lundermann rode point, setting a course that would later angle into the Apache Tank road five or six miles east of Three Links. Beauregarde, riding flank with Cliff Paddock, was kept constantly on the hop forcing the first fast-spreading bulge of cow

131

critters into some semblance of a trail herd. Snuffy steers broke from the forming line in stubborn attempts at freedom, and for a time, until the herd was strung out satisfactorily, Oscar Ellison and Pike Corvette aided in the flanking. Then, with the steers choused into order by dint of hard-swung hondas and considerable cursing, the two young riders dropped back to the drag.

Dusk's lavender light slowly deepened, running richer and fuller until it became a purple robe draping the draws and mesas and finally the mountains above them. All at once then it was dark, and night's brooding hush was broken only by a low shuffle of hoofs, creak of saddle gear and jingle of spur rowels.

Riding in the moonless gloom, Beauregarde glanced occasionally at Cliff Paddock, who was little more than a vague shadow drifting along above the moving blur of marching cattle. The Boxed P owner hadn't spoken a dozen words to Beauregarde during the past few days. Contemplating the secret animosity which there'd been between them from the moment of their first meeting, Beauregarde could only guess at Paddock's portion of that mutual dislike. But he tabbed his own part of it as a sort of envy.

The herd shuffled into the Apache Tank road, stirring up hock-deep dust into an unseen mist of acrid, irritating alkali. Beauregarde nudged up his neckerchief so that it shielded his mouth and nostrils. He heard talk up ahead and, catching the contralto tone of a feminine voice, felt an instant surge of anticipation in the thought that Susan had ridden out to visit her father. He was hoping that she'd also visit him, when a girl's dim shape loomed up in front of him and Judy Lundermann said cheerfully, 'Hello, Texican.'

Swift disappointment doused the high flare of Beauregarde's anticipation. He said, 'Howdy,' expecting that she'd continue on back to Pike Corvette.

But instead she fell in beside him and said quietly, 'I decided to do some trail herding. Aren't you glad?'

'Sure,' Beauregarde drawled, endeavoring to sound pleased and not succeeding.

Cliff Paddock called tauntingly, 'Better make it short and sweet, Judy. Moon'll be up soon and Pike might see you.'

'Tend your riding, cowpoke,' Judy retorted; then, lowering her voice, asked, 'What's the matter, Lee? Are you a woman hater, or what?'

'No,' he said. 'In fact, I'm sort of partial to 'em, Judy.'

That seemed to please her. She eased her horse in closer, so that their stirrups locked. A coyote's plaintive call drifted out of the hills, and Judy said, 'He sounds tol'able lonely, like

133

the way I feel sometimes? Don't you ever get lonesome, Lee?'

Her low woman's voice was caressingly emotional. It carried an invitation that bordered upon boldness; yet, because Beauregarde understood how insistently the little devils of discontent could prod wild impulses, he put a fair judgment on this girl's rash manner. She was, he guessed, temporarily trapped in the hidden snare of her own emotions; she was like a hot-blooded filly desiring the full freedom of open range, yet instinctively wanting the sugar she could have only in her home corral.

Fate, Beauregarde reflected, played peculiar pranks. It had brought him to Panamint Valley in search of vengeance; then, pulling the strings in frivolous fashion, had turned him loose in a crosstail tangle of guns and girls and rapacious greed; of hate and love and stubborn pride. It was enough to muddle a man's mind.

'Aren't you ever lonesome?' Judy asked again.

'Yeah,' he admitted. 'I've been lonesome as all git-out, several times.'

Whereupon she said urgently, 'You don't have to be, Texican.'

Beauregarde shaped up a cigarette. There'd been a time, and not so long ago, when this girl would have seemed entirely desirable to him; when her generous offer would have been gladly accepted. But that time had gone; all his free-lance fancies had crystallized into the deep, compact emotion a man feels for one woman, and one woman alone . . .

He said finally, 'I'm not lonesome now, Judy. But Pike might be.'

For a long moment she regarded him in shocked silence. Afterward she said, 'All right,' in a voice gone flat; gone abruptly resigned. 'All right, Texican.'

She rode back along the line of plodding steers then, and Cliff Paddock called, 'Couldn't you keep her entertained?'

'Guess not,' Beauregarde muttered, not liking to discuss a girl's romantic notions.

'Better not let Pike catch you two together,' Paddock counselled amusedly. 'He might not take kindly to competition, even from a six-gun smokeroo.'

This, Beauregarde realized, was the second time Paddock had used those words to stigmatize him with a renegade reputation. And as before, his voice was genial. If there was more than bantering behind it—if it was prompted by malicious intent or crafty insult—there was nothing in Paddock's voice to show it.

Beauregarde made no further comment. But the talk turned him to a mood of speculative thinking. What, he wondered, would be the final outcome of the trouble in Panamint

135

Valley? What would happen to Hodnett and Corvette while Three Links and the Skillet waged a war of raid and counter-raid, or ravishment and reprisal? There would come a time when no man could remain neutral, when a cowman's only chance of survival would be to choose a side and fight. Would the two ex-Pool members throw in with Blake, who had reviled their pacifist leanings; or would they hitch their hopes to an expected Skillet victory?

There were other angles equally as puzzling; equally as unsolvable at this time. What part would Sheriff Derbyshire play in the inevitable showdown? Would the lawman toss aside his frantic plans for peace and, resenting Blake's refusal to arbitrate, throw his badge in on Strebor's side?

Thinking back to the fresh-skinned hide on the O Bar E corral, Beauregarde tried to identify the reason it had seemed so familiar to him. Something about it had stirred a remote, yet prodding sense of recognition. There seemed to be something about the color; yet grulla steers were not uncommon on that range, which evidently had been stocked with Mexican-run cattle. There were cow critters of every color and every variety of marking. These old-time cattle ran the rainbow list of hues; there were duns, creams, slates, blues, blacks and brindles. There were bays with black points, white-faced reds, roan Durhams, blackpoll Anguses and humped Brahmas.

Shrugging aside the unsolvable riddle of the grulla, Beauregarde untied his buckskin jacket from behind his saddle. Night's coolness had driven the last lingering heat from the valley's floor. It would soon be downright chilly. The herd was crossing a series of undulating sand hills which bulged the desert west of a low divide of tumbled lava outcrop through which Malpais Pass made a mile-long cut to the main valley beyond.

The star-studded sky held a subdued glow, like the delicate reflection of far-off brilliance; but the moon hadn't yet topped the high wall of the Hondos and the land was still blacked out in a shroud of mealy darkness. These leggy steers made a good trail herd; once they put their minds to traveling they moved forward with mile-eating monotony. At this gait, Beauregarde calculated they should reach the stock pens at Apache Tank well before daylight. He wondered if the Elite Restaurant stayed open all night, and because he had a hankering for hot coffee, hoped the restaurant would be open . . .

Presently Dave Blake drifted back from point and, riding beside Beauregarde, asked, 'Well, what you think?'

That cryptic question roused Beauregarde from the deep preoccupation which had dulled his customary vigilance. He said, 'There wasn't

137

a sign of recent travel this side of Skyline Ridge, except the tracks Paddock made the other night. But I still don't understand it. Seems like the Skillet would have kept closer tally on us, unless—'

He was on the point of saying, 'unless Strebor had already been informed of Blake's plans, and therefore didn't need to spy.' But because his suspicion of Hank Lundermann was little more than a flimsy hunch, he didn't finish the sentence.

'Unless what?' Blake asked.

'Well,' Beauregarde evaded, 'mebbe it's as Lundermann says. Mebbe Strebor is waiting for you to force the fight.'

'I still got that funny feeling in my gizzard,' Blake muttered worriedly, 'like there was going to be a change of weather, or something.'

This talk stirred up Beauregarde's habitual wariness; it brought back the premonition that had nagged him earlier in the day. He asked, 'How far are we from Malpais Pass?'

'Two, three miles.'

'How about having Oscar come up here while I take a look-see ahead?' Beauregarde suggested. 'Pike and Judy can take care of the drag between them.'

'Sure,' Blake agreed, then added, 'We can do better than that. I'll leave Oscar back there, bring Pike up here, and have Judy ride point with Hank. Then you and me can take a look at both sides of the Pass.'

Ten minutes later Beauregarde and Blake rode on ahead of the herd and soon separated, each leaving the road at an angle which would bring them onto the divide above the pass. The moon was edging over the Hondos, when Beauregarde halted his horse on a high outcrop of jumbled lava rock. The pass was some three or four hundred yards south of him, cutting through the upheaved mass of black malpais like a man-made alleyway.

Giving the pass a lingering appraisal, Beauregarde recognized how perfect a place it would be for ambush. Drygulchers could lay in wait behind the broken boulders on either side of the gap and fire down into it without exposing themselves to any extent . . .

Beauregarde peered along the weather-carved castle of rimrock, probing their brush-blotched shadows. Then he shifted his gaze to where the strungout herd made an undulating, serpentine ribbon against the moonlit sand. A gossamer plume of trail dust billowed lazily in the windless air, and the remote rumor of steadily shuffling hoofs drifted up to him like the droning murmur of a slow-flowing stream.

Save for the herd and the gentle disturbance of its travel, there was no sign nor sound of movement anywhere. The roundabout terrain was a picture of moonlit tranquillity in a star-studded frame. Gazing out across the sand hills, Beauregarde thought he glimpsed the far-off flicker of Three Link's lighted windows. He was endeavoring definitely to identify that remote suggestion of illumination when a horse nickered somewhere below—between him and the pass!

That trivial strand of sound jerked him rigidly alert. It honed all his senses to a keen edge of expectancy. Grasping his bronc's muzzle against an answering whinny, Beauregarde focused his eyes to a probing study of the brush-fringed rimrock. There was scarcely any graze there; it was highly improbable that a loose horse would range that malpais, or the sand hills that surrounded it. This reasoning brought Beauregarde to a swift and tumultuous conclusion—to the definite understanding that there was a rider on or near the horse which had nickered. Probably several riders . . .

And that meant ambush. It meant swift slaughter of the oncoming herd, and for the riders with the herd!

As that stark realization rifled through him, Beauregarde hauled his carbine from its scabbard. And in that same instant his roving glance caught a moving glint of moonlit metal in the shadows a hundred yards ahead of him!

★   ★   ★

The Three Links herd was no more than a hundred feet from the Pass when Beauregarde thumbed back the hammer of his Henry carbine. Without shifting his gaze from those clotted shadows below, he calculated the herd's closeness by the clatter of hoofs on flinty lava—by the snorts of lead steers sniffing the rock-walled ramparts of the gap.

The glint of metal had disappeared—hidden, Beauregarde guessed, by some slight shift of a man's body. But he had marked the position of its brief appearance; he sent three fast shots into that yonder blotch of boulders and spurred his bronc to a quick jump sideways. Narrowly escaping a return volley, Beauregarde targeted yellow blooms of muzzle flame that ripped raggedly between those shadow-bordered boulders, and fired again.

He heard a man's shrilled curse, glimpsed a Skillet rider briefly outlined above the rimrock and firing with deliberate aim, then saw that toppling shape tumble backward into space. Another moving figure made a brief target, but Beauregarde's nervously fidgeting bronc spoiled his aim—and the animal's side-stepping tantrum saved Beauregarde's life. For even as he fired, he saw gun flame flare abruptly along the opposite wall of the Pass and heard a veritable hail of lead spang against the rock outcrop where he'd been a split second before.

Those yonder guns were being fired from a more advantageous angle than the ones directly below him. They were centering on him now, and they had his range perfectly. Riding behind a high-reared rampart, Beauregarde coaxed his spooked bronc to a stand and, hurriedly plucking fresh shells from his pocket, shoved them into the carbine's loading slot.

Powder smoke's acrid stench drifted plainly up to him now; the metallic ping of ricocheting slugs was like the sudden snapping of long wires, and the wild bawling of terrified cattle made a basso booming behind the continuous blast of guns. Somewhere directly below Beauregarde a man kept up a shrill, wild cursing—kept yelling, 'Dammit, git me out o' here!'

The thought occurred to Beauregarde that Dave Blake should have been in a position for a flank attack on the south side of the pass. He wondered if the old cowman could come up behind those yonderly gunhawks; if Blake could, there'd be a good chance to thwart this crafty plan to wipe out the Three Links trail herd.

And in that same instant it also occurred to Beauregarde that Judy Lundermann was riding point with her father. The significance of that startling realization brought a curse to Beauregarde's lips. The two point riders would have made plain targets for those ambush guns; Judy might already be dead, or badly wounded!

Booting his bronc up to a canted outcrop, Beauregarde peered down at the herd—and cursed again.

It was a weird, breath-taking sight. The front end of the herd had turned tail in sudden panic at the first shooting. The startled leaders had smashed head-on into the fast spreading bulge of surging, confused brutes behind them. Caught between the blast of guns in front, and the answering fire from flank and drag riders, the three hundred steers had been thrown into a milling maelstrom. The resultant tangle quickly turned into a chaotic melee of fear-maddened cattle, cursing men and lunging horses, all cloaked in a sleazy shadow of dust and drifting gunsmoke.

This much Beauregarde saw in the time it took him to loose one gusty breath. But though he glimpsed reoccurring slobbers of muzzle flame from rapidly shifting riders down there, he couldn't identify a single shape nor guess at the trail crew's remaining number. If Judy Lundermann had fallen in that dust-slurred crush of hoofs and horns, there'd be no hope for her at all . . .

Cursing the prank of fate which had brought a girl into this hellish bedlam, Beauregarde turned his attention to the Pass. The two groups of Skillet drygulchers had consolidated their positions; the original slaughter scheme spoiled by his first three shots, they'd moved forward to where they could rake the scattering herd with random slugs.

Dave Blake, Beauregarde realized abruptly, hadn't succeeded in flanking the group on the south side of the pass. But a moment later, as Beauregarde began firing at the bunched muzzle flare directly below him, another gun blazed high up on the opposite wall, and that new outburst told Beauregarde that Blake had finally joined the attack of the Skillet. Thereupon a surge of savage satisfaction boiled up like a bloodlust brew in Lee Beauregarde. Here, he knew, was a chance to smash the Skillet—the best chance Blake would ever have. Caught between two sets of guns on either side and with continuing resistance from in front, those Skillet riders were trapped in a slaughter chute of their own construction.

Backing his bronc against an overhanging shelf of rock, Beauregarde said lustily, 'Stand and shiver, jughead, while I kill off some snakes!'

He sighted the carbine with eager skill and emptied it into the body-threshed manzanita that fringed the long ledge below him. This, he thought rashly, would bring a swift and unexpected finish to the fearsome threat of wipe-out warfare in Panamint Valley. The tables were turned now; instead of coldly butchering a trapped trail herd and its riders, the Skillet's crew was itself trapped and on the defensive. The tricky fortunes of war had shifted suddenly and solidly in favor of Three Links!

That realization spurred Beauregarde's practiced fingers as he pushed fresh shells into the Henry—and heard Sid Strebor's piercing yell rise above the bullet bedlam: 'Up there—get that son up there!'

Beauregarde grinned. He targeted a skulking shape and, firing, saw the vague form fall in the peculiar final way a dead man falls. He hoped savagely that his victim had been Sid Strebor . . .

A slug slashed across Beauregarde's left cheek. Dodging instinctively away from a second slug, he pressed the raw furrow against his up-nudged shoulder. The bullet, he guessed, had cut through the v-shaped scar on his cheek. Strange that this same inch of flesh should be seared a second time; that it should be worked into a kind of brand to show where Death had clutched at him and missed on two occasions. His luck, he thought, was still good as ever. He loosed a lusty chuckle and was probing the lower ridge for another target when he glimpsed the scarlet reflection of far-off flames above the western sand hills.

For one slow motion moment, Beauregarde stared in startled bafflement. What—where was that yonder fire? Then abruptly the answer came to him; came with such smashing certainty that his blood ran cold. Not all of Strebor's gunhawks were here at Malpais Pass; some of them had raised Three Links—had set fire to it!

Susan was at Three Links—Susan, and Della Ellison, who was going to have a baby!

With that thought stabbing through him, Beauregarde slammed spurs to his bronc and rushed the grunting animal recklessly down the divide's rockstrewn shoulder. The realization that Susan and Della were probably already at the mercy of Skillet raiders put a creeping coldness in him. What if Red Valentine had been given the Three Links raid to handle? Red Valentine, who considered all women as so much shapely, sweet-scented flesh to be chased and captured . . .

All the high, hot flare for fighting vanished from Lee Beauregarde's veins. Fear crowded out the last vestige of his wild relish for conflict; fear close to being frantic. Cold, blood-chilling fear that clawed the tattered remnants of his hope, yet lashed him onward with that thin-raveled hope clutched desperately. Telling himself he would get there in time—that he *must* get there in time!

The battle here, which fleeting moments before had been so paramount, was no longer important. Whether or not the Skillet was smashed seemed trivial; whether the beef herd survived or was slaughtered didn't matter to Lee Beauregarde. Nothing was important now except this mad race toward a burning ranch—toward the only woman he had ever really wanted.

Reaching the lower slope, Beauregarde set a course that would skirt the dust-cloaked confusion of the milling beef herd. The firing still continued, and peering through drifting streamers of gunsmoke, he glimpsed three wraithlike figures weaving through the yonder fog. They, at least, had survived Skillet's bullets. He wondered if those three included Judy Lundermann, and because death seemed somehow unthinkable for so young and beautiful a girl, he hoped she was among the survivors.

★　　　★　　　★

Red Valentine and Faro Savoy stood behind the bunkhouse at Three Links, holding a council of war while the burning wagonshed sent its flame flare across the yard . . .

'There's only one gun bein' used,' Valentine argued. 'Soon as the fire dies down a little, we can rush the house easy.'

Wood smoke drifted along the wall at that point, and its acrid fumes were having their effect on Faro Savoy's diseased lungs. 'To hell with waitin',' he rasped. 'Strebor told us to blow this goddam place off the map, and if them wimmin won't come out of the house, to hell with 'em!'

He started for the dynamite-laden saddle-bags farther along the wall, but Valentine grabbed his arm. 'Ain't you got no human feelin's at all?' Red demanded. 'Ain't you got no urge to try your luck with fancy wimmin?'

'No calico is worth eatin' lead to git,' Savoy snarled impatiently, and went into another fit of coughing.

Afterward he said wheezingly, 'Them fancy dames ain't so goddam different, anyway. A Tombstone tart suits me all right. She'll give a gink his money's worth without no fuss at all.'

Valentine chuckled. 'Anythin' worth gittin' is worth fightin' for,' he declared. 'Me, I got a taste for high class calico, and I aim to have some tonight.'

★   ★   ★

Two hours of feverish, flogging, spur-prodded riding. Two seemingly endless hours while Lee Beauregarde's shadow raced him across the moonlit dust; while stubborn hope and black despair rode shoulder to shoulder like taunting, bickering companions. And with each hard-run mile his dismal thoughts ran deeper, until regret was like a lash scourging a raw sore inside him.

Why—for the first time in his gunsmoke career—had he ignored the premonition which had so insistently nagged at him? Why had he shrugged off the hunch that trouble was brewing?

And above this self-reproach was the smashing question as to why two defenseless girls had been left alone at the ranch. That seemed close to criminal negligence; with that lurid beacon of flame now plainly visible, it seemed a mistake so monstrous he couldn't comprehend how it had happened. But it had—and now he was deliberately, calculatingly killing a good horse in an effort to save those girls from being the innocent victims of that carelessness. Deftly hand-riding his horse, Beauregarde judged the animal's remaining endurance as a good physician anticipates the length of time a dying man may live—urging the animal on whenever it lagged in weariness, yet endeavoring to conserve the ebbing reservoir of its strength.

Again and again Beauregarde's mind reverted to the subtle warning his natural wariness had given him. And to the astonishing fact that he'd ignored it. He, of all men, had deliberately shunned the sixth-sense warning which so many times had been his guardian angel.

The answer, he decided, must be that his

failure to find sign of Skillet scouting had lulled him into a sense of false security. That, and the fact Hank Lundermann had impressed him with the idea that Sid Strebor was waiting for Three Links to force the fighting. Hank Lundermann—whom Beauregarde now cursed with a savage, soul-searing intensity. The thought occurred to him that Lundermann hadn't guessed his own daughter would accompany the doomed trail herd; the dirty, stinking spy hadn't anticipated that Judy would be riding point at the exact time of attack!

Climbing the east slope of Gooseneck Divide, the bronc stumbled and went to its knees. Beauregarde kept the fagged animal from falling by the sheer strength of his grip on the reins. But he knew there wasn't much more run left in his loyal, lathered horse. The poor brute was weaving on its feet, and the extended, all-out effort of its breathing was like the measured roar of a hard-worked bellows. This desperate race was more than flesh and blood could long withstand; any moment now the bronc's heart would break and the bellows would cease to function . . .

The smell of wood smoke was a plain taint on the night air. It came stronger and stronger as Beauregarde nursed his staggering mount across the crest. Wood smoke—that must mean the wagonshed, or one of the smaller buildings.

Both the main house and the bunkhouse were built of adobe. Perhaps he was still in time!

Then he heard something which sent a riot of hope surging through him—the rolling, thunderous growl of Dave Blake's big .45-.90 rifle. That meant Susan was defending the house; it meant that she'd grabbed her father's gun again, and this time she wasn't bluffing!

A Winchester's sharp bark came to Beauregarde, that lesser explosion instantly echoed by the .45-.90's roar, again and again. He urged the staggering bronc to a faster pace and, crossing the crest, sighted the ranch house weirdly illumined by the high-flaring flames of a structure behind it. Even as he watched, a great billow of smoke drifted down in breeze-blown waves that obliterated the yard in ash-gray fog. But the brief glimpse he'd had of the house reassured Lee Beauregarde to the point of blurting. 'Thank God!' with more reverence and more feeling than he'd ever used before.

He rode down the slope and urged his faltering mount to a final, desperate spurt—calling on the reserve he had so craftily hoarded against that moment. He hoped he had judged that reserve correctly . . .

The crackle of flames was plainly audible now, riding the eastward breeze like the mirthless chuckle of sardonic laughter. Beauregarde wondered how many men

Strebor had sent there, and because Susan had evidently been able to stand them off, guessed there weren't more than two at the most. It occurred to him then that they might hear him coming and block this belated arrival with bullets. But almost at once he discarded that possibility. The burning building made a continuous ripple of sound, and what little wind existed was blowing directly toward him.

Smoke stung his eyes and nostrils. It blotted out the moon. It shrouded the roundabout landscape in an opaque gloom that was neither darkness nor daylight, but a ghost-gray pall through which the yonder flames sent rose-tinted reflections. A gun roared, that rolling report like the blowing of a horn in a fog-bound harbor. And it was close ahead . . .

Then, within two hundred yards of Three Links, the bronc died on its feet. Beauregarde endeavored to jump clear, but he couldn't quite make it. The brave-hearted horse collapsed like a bursting bag, going down so suddenly that Beauregarde's right leg was wedged firmly beneath the animal's flared ribs.

For one fleeting instant, as sharp splinters of pain spiraled up his thigh, Beauregarde thought the leg was broken. But in the next moment, when he tried to pull loose, he decided the leg was merely bruised. Savagely then, cursing, with all the frantic desperation of a trapped animal struggling for freedom,

152

Beauregarde fought for release. His left leg was free, and this he used for a lever. But it wasn't enough. The bronc weighed all of twelve hundred pounds, and it was dead weight.

Another burst of firing came sharply above the crackle of flames. And then, in the ensuing lull, a voice called loudly, 'Come out of there or you'll be blown to bloody bits!'

That voice, Beauregarde knew instantly, belonged to Red Valentine!

There was a long moment then when only the sound of burning timbers came to him. He wondered if Susan had chosen to ignore the warning, and felt sure she wouldn't surrender. Except for the danger of being struck by bullets entering through the windows, the girls were comparatively safe so long as they kept Red Valentine outside.

Beauregarde was wondering about the redhead's threat to blow the girls to bloody bits when Faro Savoy's rasping yell carried across the yard: 'We got dynamite, sisters, and we're goin' to use it *muy pronto!*'

Dynamite!

That single word tied an icy knot at the pit of Beauregarde's stomach. It set him to struggling madly for release. Bracing his left foot against the saddle, he pushed and tugged and cursed in a frenzy of desperate effort. To no avail. Sweat coursed down his face. It merged with the blood that oozed from the raw furrow on his cheek, the mixture tasting salty-sweet on his lips.

Then, when he lay spent and panting, and expecting to hear a dynamite explosion at any instant, a plan came to him—a plan that might mean freedom. If he could squirm near enough to stab a knife into the dead bronc's belly, it might deflate enough to relieve the pressure on his leg!

Drawing a jackknife from his pocket, Beauregarde tugged its blade open and pushed himself up as far as his wedged leg would permit. But though he strained forward until his shin bone seemed about to snap, he wasn't near enough. Stomping down the hot tumult of fear and frustration that boiled up within him, he lay back and gave this new problem hasty consideration. All he needed was another inch or two; perhaps if he came up at a different angle he could make it . . .

Whereupon Beauregarde squirmed as far back as his leg would allow, then, twisting his body, tried again. And this time he succeeded!

Quickly then, like a man working against time, he drove the knife blade deep between two ribs and, holding it there, pressed the wound into a wider gap. For an instant he thought he hadn't stabbed deep enough—thought that the blade was too short and that his scheme had failed miserably. Then air gushed out in a steamy swish, and presently the pressure lessened on his trapped leg.

It was only a matter of minutes then until Beauregarde was on his feet and, gun in hand, was limping across the smoke-hazed yard.

From somewhere behind the dimly looming house, Red Valentine yelled again, 'This is your last chance, gals! Come out now or go up with the house!'

Swerving instantly in the direction of that voice, Beauregarde glimpsed Valentine's vague shape rounding a corner of the building. And in that same instant Beauregarde smashed solidly into Faro Savoy. The impact of collision knocked them down; the reedy gunhawk grunted as he fell, then exclaimed, 'Who are you?'

And in the next instant, as he sighted Beauregarde through the lesser smoke along the ground, Savoy tilted up his gun and fired. That half-aimed slug missed Beauregarde by inches. Spraddled full length in the dust, he swiveled hastily around—and knew Savoy wouldn't miss his second shot. But even then, with that grim knowledge coursing through him, Lee Beauregarde took time to aim deliberately . . .

Both guns exploded so nearly together that they made one continued smash of sound against the crackle of nearby flames. But even before his ears registered that double roar, Beauregarde felt the crushing impact of Savoy's slug—a slamming, shattering impact that seemed to tear his left shoulder from his body. The force of that blow knocked him off balance; it sent him slewing sideways in the dust.

And in that black moment of slug-shocked confusion, Red Valentine's voice came again: 'Faro what's up?'

That demanding query cut through the clutching pain that gripped Beauregarde like a vise. It repulsed the black boots of nausea which were tromping him into the cushioning softness of the yard's deep dust. It made him wilfully marshal all the tattered remnants of his ebbing reason—forced him into a pain-laced attempt to stand.

The thought came to him that Savoy hadn't answered Red Valentine. Glancing toward the dim heap ahead of him, Beauregarde knew that Faro Savoy would never answer—and that knowledge gave Beauregarde a savage satisfaction. The odds were even now—one to one. If there'd been more than these two gunhawks he'd have heard from them before this.

Getting groggily to his feet, Beauregarde probed the roundabout fog of wood smoke; tautly listened for the sound of footsteps. The fire behind the house was burning lower now, and slanting strands of moonlight showed through the lifting smoke haze. But there was no sight nor sound of Red Valentine.

Beauregarde was wondering about that; wondering why the redhead had so quickly given up the problem of Faro's firing, when Della Ellison's voice lifted in a startled, high-pitched scream. That cry banished the last vestige of fuzziness from Beauregarde's brain. It sent him forward in a limping run. This abrupt movement made his blood-gummed shirt tear loose from his wounded shoulder with a sucking, adhesive pull; it set up a racketing paid that ran all across his back and caused him to move forward in a lopsided, hunching stride. He was halfway across the yard when Red Valentine called puzzledly, 'That you, Faro?'

The voice came from an angle that turned Beauregarde hastily around. Valentine, he guessed, was over by the kitchen window; sight of the redhead had probably set off Della Ellison's piercing scream. The smoke was thicker there; caught in the building's long ell, it was like a flimsy fabric suspended from a high clothesline.

'Faro!' Valentine called.

Beauregarde spotted him then, an indeterminate shape a shade darker than the shadows near the kitchen doorway. But by the same token Valentine also spotted Beauregarde. Valentine's gun blasted, and a slug sizzled past Beauregarde's head as his own gun bucked against his palm. Fearful that a stray bullet might smash through a window, and so wanting a different angle for his next shot, Beauregarde limped in toward the house.

Valentine also moved, for when he fired again his gun splashed a brief gleam of orange brightness at the far corner of the house. That slug plunked into the 'dobe a full foot behind Beauregarde. It brought a twisted smile to his blood-crusted face, Valentine, he thought contemptuously, was a duck-and-dodge galoot; Skillet's redheaded foreman didn't like a stand-up fight . . .

With his dangling left arm brushing the wall, Beauregarde marched methodically along the house. There were only three shots left in his gun; and because his numb left hand was useless, reloading the weapon would be a slow and tedious chore. With this thought in mind, he held his fire, waiting for a target he might reasonably hope to hit. He pinned a tight gaze on the corner's obscure outline, and when a shadow blurred briefly there, he snapped a shot at it.

Abruptly then the rapid tromp of boots lifted above the sputter of smoldering embers beyond the house. Running forward, Beauregarde reached the corner and had one fleeting glimpse of Valentine's firelit shoulders edging around the end of the house. Whereupon

Beauregarde turned and hastily retraced his steps.

Gaining the gallery, he saw lamplight bloom yellowly in the doorway, and wondered why a lamp had been lighted, and why that door was wide open. Then he rushed across the gallery.

For one startled instant, as his eyes focused to the smoke-streamered brightness of this long room, Beauregarde stood gripped in astonishment on the doorsill. Della Ellison lay white-faced and motionless on the floor, and Susan was frantically rubbing the girl's limp wrists. Then, as Beauregarde strode inside, Susan glanced up at him with a startled stare that changed swiftly from bewilderment to wide-eyed alarm.

'Lee—you're hurt!' she cried.

Beauregarde's blood-streaked face eased into a grin. 'Not much,' he said, savoring the strange satisfaction of her instinctive sympathy. 'What's the matter with Della?'

'She fainted. I had to open the door so she could get fresh air. It was stifling in here. I—I guess I made a mistake setting fire to the wagon-shed, Lee—but it kept them from sneaking across the backyard.'

'Sure—sure,' Beauregarde agreed, feeling a high surge of appreciation for this girl's courage. Then, remembering that Red Valentine was skulking around somewhere, he backed hastily toward the doorway. 'There's still one skunk out there I've got to find,' he muttered.

'Oh, Lee—we've got to get a doctor for Della!' Susan exclaimed. 'She's going to have a baby—tonight!'

And in that same instant, as Beauregarde glanced down at the stricken young wife who was on the verge of motherhood, Red Valentine snarled, 'Drop that gun, Texican—and drop it quick!'

CHAPTER SIX

Lee Beauregarde stood frozen, not by fear of himself, but by fear for Susan, who stood directly in front of him. He couldn't whirl and fire fast enough to keep Valentine from slamming a shot this way—and that slug might hit Susan!

'Come on, come on,' Valentine ordered. 'Make up your mind.'

It was, Beauregarde realized, an almost hopeless decision, whichever way he chose. There was just an outside chance he would live long enough to kill the blocky-faced gunhawk behind him—but there was also the chance that such an attempt might turn this room into a bloody shambles.

Deciding against such a risk to Susan and Della, Beauregarde let the gun slip from his fingers, and instantly felt the sense of utter futility a gunfighter feels without a gun. Turning slowly, he faced Red Valentine, and saw the gloating grin that creased the redhead's cheeks.

'I'm rememberin' something,' Valentine declared. 'I'm rememberin' the first time me and you met our blonde lady friend. You said she wasn't my kind, remember? And you said she didn't have no more warmth than winter sun on a snow drift.'

Beauregarde nodded. He calculated the distance between them. Valentine was standing just inside the front doorway, seven or eight feet away—maybe ten. Too far for a man with a lame leg to jump. But the lamp was nearer. It was on a table near enough to reach in one swift lunge, and that lunge would take him away from Susan. She wouldn't be a target then . . .

'Well,' Valentine continued, visibly enjoying the moment, 'I didn't agree with you that day, Texican. And I ain't agreein' now. I got me a hunch she's not cold at all. Not when she's handled right, and I'm the gink can handle 'em. But first me and you has a little business to do outside, Texican.'

His voice turned sly with mock politeness. 'You wouldn't want it done in here, would you, friend Beauregarde? You wouldn't want

161

Blondie to see how unhandsome a galoot looks with his mouth hangin' open like a burro with the heaves.'

Beauregarde knew what he meant. He could see the slaughter glint in Valentine's muddy eyes—the crooked, smirking smile that slanted across Valentine's roan cheeks. Red had looked like this that day he'd killed the jackrabbit out on the flats.

'You like your meat all propped for slaughter, don't you?' Beauregarde taunted, tapping his empty holster.

The redhead chuckled. 'Yeah—that and blonde wimmin. Come on, Texican. Come on out in the moonlight. You'll look real nice, layin' alongside Faro.'

Sudden recognition of what this talk inferred brought a shocked exclamation to Susan's lips. 'No—no, you can't kill him in cold blood! You can't!'

Valentine chuckled. 'I could,' he said amusedly, 'but I won't—not in here. Come on outside, Texican.'

'No,' Susan cried, 'no—please! I'll—I'll go with you, if that's what you want.'

Beauregarde thought he must be dreaming. He thought the grasping fingers that clawed at his blood-sapped body must have garbled his hearing. He couldn't believe that what he heard was real—couldn't comprehend that any girl would make such an offer to save a man.

It couldn't be real—yet it was. He could see its stark reality in Susan's fear-blanched face and in the startled stare of her blue eyes. She was offering herself to this grinning calico chaser—to the very brute she'd fought off so desperately!

'I ain't in a bargainin' mood tonight,' Valentine declared. 'This here Texican is an outlaw, Blondie. He's wanted by the sheriff, and also by my boss, who is a reg'lar fanatic for law and order. Sid put a five hundred dollar bounty on Beauregarde's hide, which same I'm fixin' to collect. After that little chore is finished, me and you will talk things over, private-like.'

There was no mercy in him, nor any carelessness. His hot eyes didn't leave Beauregarde, even while he talked to Susan. And because Beauregarde had tallied Valentine's killer character that day a week ago, he understood that all the talking in the world wouldn't change Red's mind; no pleading would penetrate his thick-skinned brutality, nor turn him from his grisly purpose. He was like a blood-lusting animal, with fangs bared and slobbering. He would execute an unarmed man as unhesitatingly as he had butchered that burro on the flats, and he'd take his way with a defenseless girl equally as quickly.

The stark realization of Susan's danger

163

caused Beauregarde to take a tighter hold on himself, to fight off the weakness that kept clutching at his ebbing strength. His shoulder was bleeding steadily, and the thought came to him that he'd lost a lot of blood. Too much. His whole side was drenched with it; sticky, warmly wet with it. Blood ran down his left arm and dripped from his numb fingers like red sweat . . .

'No, Blondie—don't go near that rifle!' Valentine ordered; and, turning, Beauregarde saw Susan stooping with one hand poised for reaching toward the big .45-.90 that lay on the floor just beyond her . . .

'I wouldn't shoot a good-lookin' gal like you, Blondie—not unless I had to,' Valentine cautioned. 'But don't make no grab toward that gun or I'll have to.'

Della Ellison propped herself up on an elbow, asking dazedly, 'What happened?'

Beauregarde didn't look at her. He couldn't. And he couldn't look at Susan. Marshaling every ounce of strength left in him, he made ready for the thing he had to do—the only thing left for him to do. It was, he reflected, a peculiar way for a six-gun smokeroo to die. But it was better than being butchered like a steer in a slaughter chute. Even though he might not live long enough to smash that lamp and get the fingers of his good hand around Valentine's throat, he could make the try . . .

'Come on, chum,' Valentine invited. 'Let's you and me step outside. It won't take long.'

Susan had knelt beside Della again, and was urgently coaxing her to lie down. Hearing Della's low groaning, Beauregarde cursed the gimmick game Fate had framed for him. He should have been riding for a doctor now, instead of standing there waiting to die. A medico could ease that poor girl's suffering—could safeguard the new life so soon to be ushered into that smoke-tainted room.

He said savagely, 'Valentine—you're a dirty, stinking dog!'

And he was making ready to lunge at the lamp when Cliff Paddock's burly shape loomed in the doorway behind Valentine . . .

'Hoist 'em!' Paddock commanded.

Astonishment ripped all expression from Valentine's face. It wiped away the gloating grin; it blanked his eyes and bulged them wide, and it stampeded him into thoughtless action. With one spasmodic motion he ducked and whirled.

Paddock's gun exploded. Once, twice, then a third time—the shots came so close together there was scarcely any break between them. That vicious repetition of room-trapped sound tinkled a bell of ironic reflection in Beauregarde's brain—made him recall the wanton way Valentine had once killed a little boy's burro. 'The three-bullet brand,'

Valentine had called it. And now Paddock had burned him with that same killer brand.

All this occurred in the fleeting moment while Beauregarde's muscles relaxed and his whole body went slack. A wave of numbness ran through him, rising higher and higher, until it muffled his mind against the burning core of pain in his shoulder. Until it did something to his eyes, so that he lost sight of Valentine's crumpling bulk over there by the door. He heard the impact of Valentine's body on the floor. The sound seemed to come from a long way off—and as if in echo, Susan's glad exclamation rang out: 'Cliff, you came just in time!'

But the black boots of nausea were tromping on him again. They were stomping on his shoulders like huge hammers, beating him down. The floor was tilting up in crazy fashion, and he was bracing himself against losing his balance. It was almost comical the way the room was careening all topsy-turvy, with the floor boards bouncing up until they struck him in the face.

Bright sprays of dazzling light spiraled in tinsel splendor before Beauregarde's eyes—beautiful, sparkling lights. For a short time, while he floated out on an ebb tide of gentle rippling water, there was the sound of distant voices. One of them was Susan's voice, and she was calling his name. But presently the lights and the voices vanished.

And then there was nothing at all . . .

★　　　★　　　★

Sheriff Sam Derbyshire was heading for his usual early breakfast at the Elite Restaurant when Cliff Paddock rode a staggering, sweat-lathered horse down Main Street at daybreak. Even before Paddock pulled up in front of the Mercantile Building, Sheriff Derbyshire guessed why he was there; and guessing, stood gripped in grim expectancy.

'What's wrong?' he demanded.

Paddock jumped from his horse, rubbing sweat from his face with a swipe of his sleeve. 'All hell broke loose last night,' he declared, and hurried across the sidewalk. 'Big fight at Malpais Pass, and another at Three Links.'

He rushed up the outside stairway to Doc Dulaine's office and pounded on the door.

Little Joe Fagan came running from the livery stable. He joined Derbyshire at the foot of the stairway and called up to Paddock, 'Anybody killed?'

'Hell yes,' the Boxed P owner blurted. 'Two Skillet riders at Three Links; Hank Lundermann, and God knows how many more at the Pass. Better get a wagon out there to bring 'em in.'

The door opened and Paddock said urgently,

'Hurry up, Doc. Bunch of bullet wounds waiting for you, and Della Ellison needs you bad too. Susan says she's going to have her baby right soon.'

Doc Dulaine stepped out on the landing, looking like a rotund cherub in his underwear. 'Joe, hitch up my rig quick,' he said. 'I'll be right down.'

Fagan ran back to the livery, and Paddock joined Sam Derbyshire at the Elite counter for a cup of coffee. 'How'd it start?' the lawman asked.

'Strebor's bunch was waiting for us at the Pass. Dave and Beauregarde went on ahead and spoiled their play. While the fight was on I happened to see the reflection of a fire off to the west. Well, I figgered what that might mean, and hightailed it for Three Links. Found Beauregarde all shot up, with Red Valentine holding a gun on him.'

'What happened then?' the sheriff asked.

'Well, I told Red to hoist, but instead he threw down on me, or tried to. It was either him or me. The damn fool went loco, I reckon. He was threatenin' Susan when I came up behind him.'

Derbyshire eyed him thoughtfully. 'What happened then?' he asked.

'Beauregarde passed out, and Della had already fainted. I hated like hell to leave Susan alone in a mess like that, but she said

168

Della had to have Doc right away, so I headed for town. On the way in I met Dave and the others going back to the ranch. They'd blasted hell out of Strebor's bunch, but Lundermann is dead, Pike Corvette is dying, and Dave has a busted arm. Judy was with us on the drive. She's riding double with Pike, holding him up in saddle, and crying like a baby.'

Sheriff Derbyshire took a long swig of coffee. His angular face tightened into a deep furrowed scowl, and he said slowly, 'I didn't want to see it happen. But it has, by God, and I can't stand by no longer.'

His big-knuckled fingers unpinned the star on his vest, and for a hushed moment he looked at the badge in the way a man might look at a departing friend—at an old and cherished friend. Then he laid the star on the counter and announced, 'I'm quitting the sheriff's job.'

'Why?' Paddock demanded, wholly puzzled.

'A sheriff can't take sides,' Derbyshire said slowly, choosing his words. 'Long as he wears that badge he's got to go right down the middle, showing no partiality. But I ain't sheriff no longer. I'm free to do what I please, so I'm siding Dave. And unless I miss my guess I'll have Jeb Hodnett and Tate Corvette with me from here on. Sid Strebor overstepped himself tonight, and he'll find it out goddam soon!'

169

Paddock smiled wryly, saying, 'Reckon he found it out already.'

Joe Fagan came into the restaurant. 'Doc's gone,' he reported. 'Says for you to bring in the dead ones and he'll do his coroner duty on 'em when he gets back. I got a wagon all hitched.'

Derbyshire pointed to the badge. 'I ain't the law around here no more, Joe. But I'll help you bring in the bodies. After that I'm going to reorganize the Panamint Pool for Dave Blake.'

This announcement didn't seem to surprise the little liveryman at all. 'I been wonderin' how long it'd take you to see the light,' he drawled grinningly and, reaching up, slapped the lanky ex-lawman on the shoulder. 'Hell, we'll all sign up with the Pool now. You and me, Gus Lorillard and Con Dooly. It'll be stronger than it ever was, won't it, Cliff?'

'Sure,' Paddock agreed. 'And I'd hate to be in Strebor's boots—if he's still alive.' Then he asked, 'Say, you got a bottle over at the barn, Joe? I need a shot of whiskey before I ride to TC and tell 'em about Pike.'

Fagan nodded understandingly. 'I'd hate to face Orphelia Corvette with less than three drinks under my belt,' he declared. 'She set a lot o' store by young Pike—thought he was about the greatest kid that ever lived. She'll take on somethin' terrible.'

Sam Derbyshire gave Paddock a reflective

170

glance, seeing how thoroughly shaken he was. 'You ride back to Three Links,' the old lawman said. 'I'll take the word to the Corvettes.'

★　　★　　★

Morning sunlight swept westward across Panamint Valley. It gilded the jagged ramparts of Malpais Divide where scattered cartridge cases glinted brassily against the black lava, and blood stains smeared the brush. It crept down the rocky slants to where a great flock of buzzards, gorged and sluggish, perched on bloody mounds of trampled steer meat.

A strict hush, like the shocked silence after howling tumult, hung over this desolate scene of recent conflict—a hush broken occasionally by a whir of wings as additional scavengers swooped down to join the ghoulish feast.

Five miles eastward Joe Fagan drove a creaking wagon toward Apache Tank; a wagon laden with the death-stiffened bodies of six Skillet riders and Hank Lundermann . . .

Ben Smith shared the seat with Fagan. His big hands held the twisted ends of a tourniquet fashioned tightly about his right thigh. He said dazedly, 'It was the dam'dest thing I ever seen. There was guns poppin' all around us.'

'Sid Strebor won't be talkin' so goddam loud for a spell,' Fagan prophesied. He squirted

171

tobacco juice at a fly on the off-horse's hip and said hopefully, 'There can't be more'n three-four of you Skillet riders left.'

Smith grunted agreement. 'Beat hell how Strebor made such a mistake. Looks like his spy must've double-crossed him or somethin'.'

'Who's his spy?' Fagan asked casually, as if that knowledge were of little importance to him.

'Nobody seems to know that except Sid himself,' Smith muttered, and took another turn on the blood-soaked scarf around his leg. 'I'm foggin' to hell out of this valley on the next stage to Tombstone. Sid pays high wages, but he ain't payin' enough to keep me after what I seen last night. Them Three Links boys really poured it on us!'

Farther south, on a mesquite flat between Tate Corvette's place and the Spear H, Jeb Hodnett glimpsed a riderless horse standing above a spraddled shape in the dust. Deserting the ring-wormed calf he'd been chasing, Hodnett rode close enough to identify the Skillet brand on the ground-hitched bronc, and a moment later recognized Dakota Dawson's pain stricken face.

Dawson's eyes were open. He hunched up on an elbow as Hodnett hastily dismounted. His right hand clutched the blood-soaked mess his shirt made across his stomach, and he croaked, 'Water!' in a crazy, whining voice.

172

Hodnett turned to his saddle and unstripped a canteen; he was holding it to Dakota's fever-blistered lips when the gun-shot gunhawk died. And while Hodnett stood there, staring at the foolish grin on Dawson's face, he heard the plodding tromp of a nearby horse.

Getting quickly up, Hodnett watched a dust-peppered black bronc stop fifteen feet away with a bald-headed rider slung sackwise across its saddle. Blood blotched the back of the rider's shirt; blood ran down his neck and fanned out in web-like rivulets across his hairless head; it made dust-caked clots across his dangling, slack-jawed face.

'Baldy Severide,' Hodnett muttered in awesome wonderment.

And while he stood there staring at those stark symbols of gunsmoke carnage, the morning sun continued its methodical march across the quiet range. It warmed the tree-bordered meadows of the Draggon Hills; it put a coppery shine on the 'dobe walls of the Three Links ranch house where Doc Dulaine held a newborn baby by the heels. The perspiring medico spanked the infant into crying, and presently leaving the bedroom, announced, 'It's a boy!'

Oscar Ellison exclaimed, 'Golly!' in a husky, high-strung voice. He rubbed the blond stubble of whiskers on his face and grinned. 'A son,' he said solemnly.

This was Friday morning—before Sheriff Derbyshire had carted off the bodies of Red Valentine and Faro Savoy.

★   ★   ★

Later, a long time later, Lee Beauregarde became remotely aware of voices. He endeavored to push back the strange blanket of weariness that shrouded all his senses—tried to pierce the sleazy murk of unreal shadows creeping across his eyes. Once, when a pure white flame of pain stabbed his shoulder, he heard a man's voice close beside him and felt the probing of a man's fingers. But because he was trying to push away the fuzzy, quilted fog that shrouded him, Beauregarde had only a detached interest in those things.

Afterward he recognized Susan's voice saying, 'But, Doc, he's been like this for almost twelve hours! Are you sure he's going to be all right!'

'Sure I'm sure,' a man said crisply. 'It's shock, and loss of blood. He'll be coming around any time now.'

When Beauregarde opened his eyes he saw familiar objects: the peeling plaster of the bunkhouse wall, and his own duffle sack suspended from a rafter where pack rats couldn't get at it.

Almost at once then the fuzzy stuff ebbed

away, and he saw that Susan was kneeling beside the bunk . . .

'Doc was right!' she exclaimed happily. 'You've just been sleeping!'

'Yeah,' Beauregarde drawled and, hunching up, felt the strapped tightness of a bandage across his left shoulder.

He had his first full view of the room then, and perceived Orphelia Corvette's huge shape in front of a bunk diagonally across from him. She was placing a dripping towel on Pike's forehead.

'What's wrong with Pike?'

'Fractured skull,' Susan said quietly.

For a full moment Beauregarde stared at that yonder bunk in puzzlement. Then abruptly he remembered the fight at Malpais Pass, the wild ride to Three Links, and Cliff Paddock's timely arrival. 'How about the others?' he asked quickly. 'Did Judy get hurt?'

He saw a queer expression come into Susan's eyes—a peculiar, different expression that he'd never seen in them before. She said, 'No, Judy didn't get a scratch. But her father was killed.'

'So?' Beauregarde mused, feeling relief that Judy had escaped, and a sort of grim satisfaction that Hank Lundermann had paid a just price for his spying treachery . . .

'How about your dad, and Oscar?' he asked.

'Dad's right arm was shattered, but Oscar wasn't hurt at all. And he's proud as a peacock because he's the father of a baby boy.'

She got up then and stood for a moment quietly regarding him. Her eyes still held that queerly indefinable expression: a sort of harassed, worried look. 'I'm glad that Cliff came when he did,' she said presently. 'I hate to think what would've happened to us. You'd have been killed, and there'd been no doctor for Della.'

It occurred to Beauregarde then what an enormous difference Paddock's coming had made, and what a monstrous debt he owed to the Boxed P owner. For, although Susan wasn't mentioning it, she also had been saved from something—something she didn't want to talk about, and which he didn't want to think about. But recognition of that knowledge was in her eyes now, for they turned warmly reflective . . .

'Cliff couldn't have timed it better,' she added.

'He saved us all,' Beauregarde said, and realized suddenly that those four words were a brief farewell to his high hopes of romance. He guessed also the significance of the expression in Susan's eyes.

She nodded and, smiling gently, said, 'A great deal has happened since we rode through the pines yesterday, Lee. More than I ever dreamed could happen in so short a time.'

It was, he thought instantly, her way of

176

telling him how her feelings had changed toward Cliff Paddock. Not changed, exactly, for she'd held much more than a casual interest for Paddock. But last night's dramatic occurrences had fanned that interest to a fuller flame. She'd been free yesterday; now she was no longer free. And because Paddock had unquestionably saved his life, Lee Beauregarde's freedom was also curtailed. Trying to take a girl away from a man you didn't especially like could be a thoroughly enjoyable contest; but making the same try against a man who'd saved your life was another thing entirely—an almost unthinkable thing . . .

And while these thoughts raced swiftly, morosely through his mind, Beauregarde was aware of Susan's speculative gaze. It was as if she were waiting for some admission of understanding; waiting for him to acknowledge acceptance of the change which had taken place. Or so he thought.

Their glances met and held. In that hushed interval Lee Beauregarde put a deep and deliberate reckoning on the gifts this girl could give a man. She was the rich fulfillment of his every desire; his every wish. She fed all his senses. She was food and drink and warmth and fragrance; she was sunshine, shadow and melody. These were the precious things he was losing—the gifts he had already lost.

He said finally, 'Yes, Susan. A great deal happened.'

And because this was another turn in the twisted trail Fate had snapped for him to follow, Beauregarde's lips eased into a mirthless, fatalistic grin. 'Too many things happened in too short a time,' he added.

Orphelia Corvette's grief-choked voice lanced sharply across the room. 'Can't you two be quiet?' she complained. 'Can't you stop that jabbering for a while?'

Susan nodded at the stand beside Beauregarde's bunk. 'There's fresh water in the pitcher,' she said softly. 'I'll go make you some coffee.'

She went out then, her sunlit shadow lingering for an instant on the doorstep. Watching that shadow fade, Beauregarde felt all his high hopes fade with it—and knew a more dismal sense of loss than he'd ever known before.

Slumping back on the bed, he stared up at the cobwebbed ceiling, his body perfectly still, favoring the soreness of bullet-torn muscles and the strained ligaments in his legs. But there was no stillness in his mind, nor any relaxation. His thoughts kept turning back, kept reverting to that brief glimpse of a man's glory he'd been given yesterday afternoon up in the pines. It had been, he judged, about this same time of day . . .

What a monstrous difference twenty-four hours had made. In that brief space of time blood had been spattered all through the hills. There'd been black treachery, and dramatic deliverance; there'd been death and birth and painful wounds galore. This time yesterday he'd been high in spirit, filled with rash expectancy; now he had only a memory of what might have been—a glimpsed glory to remember in the frugal warmth of lonely campfires on all the dark nights to come.

And into this dismal parade of futile reflections slipped an ironic realization. He'd once told Cliff Paddock that no matter who won a range war, everybody lost. Well, Paddock hadn't lost in this war; he'd won the love and admiration of the grandest girl in the world—and he'd probably never know how close he had come to losing her.

A drone of voices drifted in from the yard. Beauregarde heard Dave Blake ask, 'How about Beauregarde, Doc? Is he going to be laid up long?'

'No, I don't think so. The bullet barely grazed a bone. It ripped right on through his shoulder muscles, making a good clean hole. He lost a lot of blood, but he's tough as Texas rawhide. He'll be up and doing directly.'

Up and doing . . .

That, Beauregarde reflected, was one way of chousing the sense of loss and futility from his mind. Abruptly then the need for movement, became a prodding, motivating need. Hunching up on his elbows, he saw that his shirt was draped over the back of a nearby chair; his boots and socks were handy on the floor. And because Orphelia Corvette kept glancing at him, Beauregarde was thankful that Doc Dulaine hadn't removed his riding pants.

He was making a one-armed attempt at getting into his shirt when Judy Lundermann came in with a cup of coffee.

'What are you trying to do?' she demanded.

Beauregarde grinned and said, 'I was figgering to get some clothes on.' And when she'd helped him into the shirt, he added, 'Thanks, Judy. Thanks a lot.'

She handed him the coffee, and he noticed that her eyes were wet with recently shed tears. Until right then he'd thought those brown eyes of hers had a permanent twinkle—a kind of teasing, taunting laughter that was as much a part of them as their color. But they were without luster now, and her face held a wistful, subdued expression . . .

He drank the coffee. Then he said, 'I'm sorry you had to lose your father, Judy. It's a hard thing to take.'

'I—I keep remembering how I forced him into siding Dave Blake,' she confessed, close to tears. 'It never occurred to me that he'd be killed—that I was hounding him to his death.'

Then she added, 'At least he didn't suffer, which is one thing I can be thankful for. Poor Dad never knew what struck him.'

She turned toward the door, and on the way, hesitated beside Mrs. Corvette. 'How is Pike?' she asked urgently.

The big woman didn't look at her. For a moment Beauregarde thought Mrs. Corvette was going to ignore the question completely. Then she said in a flat, resigned voice, 'Doc says he's going to make it. But I don't know. He ain't never opened his eyes—mebbe he never will.'

Beauregarde was tugging on his boots. He said confidently, 'Sure he will. He'll make it, ma'am.'

Whereupon Orphelia Corvette turned on him with all the unreasoning savagery of a lioness at bay. 'Pike's blood is on your head,' she accused. 'There'd've been no fighting if you'd gone to jail where you belong. You're to blame—you and this sweet-eyed flirt who took Pike away from me with her wanton kisses!'

Judy went to the doorway without speaking, and because there was no single word of defense in him, Beauregarde didn't speak either. This, he thought grimly, was part of the picture range wars always painted. And it was another price a six-gun smokeroo had to

pay—part of the bitterness he'd taken with him
when he rode on down the trail.

★　　　★　　　★

Sam Derbyshire helped Gus Lorillard dispatch
his duties as undertaker, and when the nine
bodies had been prepared for burial, said
prophetically, 'There'll be another for you to
work on tomorrow, Gus.'

'Who?' the merchant asked.

'Well, I'm not sure,' Derbyshire muttered,
and gazed thoughtfully at the wrinkled
envelope he'd taken from Red Valentine's
hip pocket. 'But I'm hoping it's Sid Strebor.'

★　　　★　　　★

Lee Beauregarde slouched in an easy chair on
the gallery at Three Links, listening to the
drawling, deliberate talk of the men gathered
there that Friday afternoon. The women and
children were inside eating supper, and that
fact in itself was significant . . .

Dave Blake roosted on the railing with his
right arm in a sling. He said, 'My beef drive
wasn't so much of a bust at that, the way
things turned out. We lost one good man, and
Pike got hurt bad, but, by God, we put a big
crimp in Strebor's crew!'

Jeb Hodnett and Tate Corvette both nodded

agreement and, watching them Beauregarde sensed a fuller, more fundamental significance in their attitude. These two men were no longer woman-counselled pacifists. They'd ridden in at noon bringing their saddle guns.

Cliff Paddock said, 'Not more'n two or three Skillet riders got out of it alive with Strebor.'

Paddock too, had a different way with him. His voice held a sober, subdued tone; there was less indolent humor in him. Placing a tentative judgment on this, Beauregarde guessed that Paddock was feeling the importance of a man hailed as a hero. The story of his timely and efficient elimination of Red Valentine had been repeated by Blake to each new arrival. He was, Beauregarde reflected, as near to being a White Knight today as a mortal man could be.

'What you plan to do now, Dave?' Hodnett inquired. 'How you figgerin' to wind it up?'

A rash eagerness brightened Blake's faded eyes. 'We're going to wind it up at daybreak tomorrow,' he reported. 'Sam Derbyshire is coming out here tonight. Joe Fagan, Gus Lorillard and Honest John are meeting us at Skyline Spring at three o'clock in the morning. Then we ride south.'

'You goin' to burn Skillet?' Oscar Ellison inquired.

Blake nodded. 'But not until we've strung Sid Strebor to a rafter,' he declared.

Presently they trooped into the supper table,

183

and there again the talk ran into retribution and reprisal. There were no dissenting voices now; no suggestions of diplomacy nor mention of fearsome consequences. Orphelia Corvette strode ponderously back to her vigil at Pike's bedside, relieving Susan, who thereafter joined Judy Lundermann in Della's room.

Finished with his one-handed eating, Beauregarde eased back in his chair and listened to the mounting violence of these men's voices. Of them all, Dave Blake was the least changed; he was still the arrogant old war chief brewing plans for swift conquest. Young Oscar Ellison's voice held a prideful note of fatherhood, and Jeb Hodnett was like a man who'd contrived to break some shackling bond long endured. But the change in Tate Corvette was more pronounced. This once meek little man had undergone a transformation so complete that even his voice was altered; no longer meek nor faltering, his tone carried a full cargo of eager anticipation . . .

'Why wait for tomorrow morning?' Corvette demanded. 'We don't need no additional help. There's four of us, not counting Beauregarde. Why don't we start for the Skillet right now?'

Beauregarde expected Cliff Paddock's quick seconding of this motion. But it didn't come. And Dave Blake said sternly, 'This isn't just a Pool affair now. Those others have a right to join in something that's for the good of

Panamint Valley. We'll wait for them like we planned.'

'Hangin' is too damn good for that dirty son Strebor!' Corvette declared. 'If my boy dies I'll cut Strebor's heart out and feed it to the hogs!'

Sitting there, Beauregarde felt entirely out of it. These men were fired by various embers of revenge, good citizenship and pride in protecting their community. But he had none of that to heat his blood, nor whet his appetite for further conflict. The Pool's need for him was ended; his debt of gratitude to Dave Blake was paid, and he was once again just a gun-smoke pariah about to pull his picket pin and drift . . .

So thinking, he pushed back his chair and, standing up, glanced at Dave Blake. 'You going to need me tomorrow morning?' he asked quietly.

'No,' Blake said. 'You're in no condition for fighting.'

And Jeb Hodnett drawled, 'This is sort of a community affair, Beauregarde. Something we should've done before you ever got here.'

A thin, ironic smile quirked Beauregarde's lips. There was nothing left for him here at all. His part was played. He said, 'Reckon I'll mosey into town. Feel the need of a bottle coming on.'

'No use to make that long ride,' Blake said quickly. 'I got a quart of Colonel Monogram in the medicine chest and you're welcome to it, Lee.'

Beauregarde shook his head, and drawled grinningly, 'Always did my drinking in a saloon. It's a habit I wouldn't care to break.'

Whereupon he sauntered out to the gallery steps and took time clumsily to fashion a cigarette. The tight bandage around his shoulder had caused a wooden numbness that reached all the way to the fingers in his left hand. But except for a throbbing ache in the high muscles of his back and a washed out, empty sort of weakness that the supper hadn't relieved, he felt fit enough.

Catching his private bronc in the corral, Beauregarde managed the tedious chore of what amounted to one-armed saddling, then went to the bunkhouse and retrieved his warbag.

Mrs. Corvette glanced up as he passed. She said forlornly, 'I'm sorry for what I said. I—I just couldn't help it. You'll have to forgive me.'

Tears streamed down her heavy cheeks, and in that moment she looked smaller, more feminine and pitiful than he'd thought so large a woman could look. He was completely sorry for her.

'You had a right to say it,' he declared and, shifting his glance to the composed, boyish features of young Pike, added, 'I've got a hunch he's going to make it, ma'am—in fact, I'm sure he will.'

Her mobile, tear-stained face smiled up at him then, and though it was a strange thing for a six-gun smokeroo to have, this was the picture Lee Beauregarde carried with him as he rode across the Three Links yard at a walk. Fate, he reflected, played damned queer pranks on a man. One woman, recently hating all he stood for, wishing him Godspeed, while another so recently in his arms, was being cheated of a chance even to say goodbye . . .

He was almost to the gate when Oscar Ellison came running out and said, 'We've just decided something.'

Beauregarde waited, wholly puzzled and impatient to leave the yard without the necessity of farewells. If Ellison noticed the warbag tied behind the saddle, he'd know this was no mere trip to town for a drink . . .

But Ellison didn't notice. He announced, 'We've named my son.'

His use of the word 'my' stirred a faint amusement in Beauregarde. Here, he decided, was a thoroughly proud and happy man.

'We've named him Lee Beauregarde Ellison,' the young father continued. 'It was Della's idea.'

That news surprised and pleased Beauregarde. It was, he knew, a reward for his Good Samaritan act that first day in Apache Tank—for the nearest thing to deliberate meddling he'd ever done.

He said, 'That's fine. Tell your wife I appreciate the honor, that I'm hoping she and the baby get along fine.'

Then he added, 'Reckon I better be going. I've got a considerable thirst.'

Ellison grinned in comradely fashion, said, 'Don't fall overboard, Lee,' and turned back to the house.

Beauregarde rode on across the flats, bracing himself against the jarring notion of the horse and not glancing back until he topped Gooseneck Divide at dusk. There he halted briefly, scanning the distant twinkle of windowlight and remembering the other times he'd stopped there. There'd been that first night when Susan had been with him, and yesterday afternoon with the sense of her arms and lips a real and tangible presence beside him. Even last night, when he'd caught that smoke-smudged glimpse of Three Links, fear and hope had been bickering companions riding with him, and so he hadn't been alone. But now he *was* alone.

Riding on across the dusk-shrouded ridge, Beauregarde glimpsed an approaching rider on the road and watched him with a casual indifference. The ebb and flow of traffic in the valley no longer interested nor concerned him. Panamint Valley's riders could come and go any way they pleased; they could stand on their heads for all he gave a damn. The book here was closed for him, and there remained only the necessity of forgetting its one bright page . . .

Sam Derbyshire came along in leisurely fashion and halted in front of Beauregarde. 'Thought you wouldn't be riding before tomorrow,' he said surprisedly.

Beauregarde was in no mood for idle chatter. He said, 'Well, I'm riding,' and added maliciously, 'Mebbe I'll blotch a brand or two before the moon comes up.'

'What the hell you talkin' about?' Derbyshire demanded.

'Seems like I remember you trying to arrest me for changing a Skillet into an O Bar E,' Beauregarde muttered. 'Do you still think I did that job?'

'No—and I never did think so. I had a hunch who did it, but hunches ain't enough. Thought mebbe I could smoke out the real blotcher by hangin' it on you.'

Recalling his own hunch about Lundermann, and again inwardly cursing himself for not having acted on that hunch in time, Beauregarde asked, 'Did you suspect a Skillet rider?'

Derbyshire shook his head. 'Leastwise he wasn't supposed to be on Strebor's payroll. But that ain't sayin' as how he wasn't receivin' some sort of pay from the Skillet.'

'Mebbe we've got the same hunch. Somebody tipped off Strebor to Blake's beef drive. The man who did that also handled the brand blotching.'

'Shouldn't wonder,' the lawman declared. 'I shouldn't wonder none at all if your hunch was right.'

Then he dug a dog-eared letter from his pocket and handed it over, saying, 'Found this in Red Valentine's pocket. I remembered you sayin' you was lookin' for a man named Roberts, so I fetched it along.'

Beauregarde opened the pencil-scrawled letter. It said:

Hear you're hanging out in Lincoln. If you're still there when this reaches you, I've got a deal that you'll be glad to hear about. Real money in it for you, Red, so come arunning. This Panamint Valley is about the slickest piece of cow country you ever seen, and it will be a cinch for one strong outfit to take over. I've got the biggest ranch here—the Skillet. If you want to take a hand in this play, there's top fighting wages and a bonus when I bust up the Panamint Pool. If you've got any friends that know how to trip a trigger, bring them along.

'Sid Roberts.

'*P.S. On account of some marshal trouble in Texas, I'm going under the name of Strebor, which is Roberts spelled backwards.*'

Roberts. Marshal trouble in Texas!
The smashing significance of that slugged its way into Beauregarde's brain. S T R E B O R . . . the same letters his father had traced in the dust with a dying finger; the same seven letters in reverse!

'You reckon he's the Roberts you been lookin' for?' Derbyshire asked.

'Yes,' Beauregarde muttered in a voice gone cold, gone thin and brittle as broken glass. 'Yes—he's the gut-shooting bastard I've trailed for three tough years.'

Again, as on that other day when Red Valentine had crowded him, something touched Beauregarde's features and changed them. The angular planes of his face grew taut; toughness traced its rippling bulge along his cheekbones and temper flared its smoky banners in his eyes. He asked, 'Has Strebor been in town today?'

'No. Reckon he's stickin' close to the Skillet, along with Ace-High Gregg, who's all the crew Sid has left.'

Beauregarde said, 'Thanks for bringing me the letter. It's the best news I've had in a long, long time. I'm much obliged.'

He turned his horse off the road and was

heading southward when Derbyshire called, 'You goin' to Skillet now?'

Beauregarde nodded.

'Want me to mosey along with you?' Derbyshire asked.

'No, I guess not,' Beauregarde muttered. 'This is a sort of personal deal that I'd like to handle alone.'

Sam Derbyshire sighed and, continuing on toward Three Links, called, 'Good luck, son—you're liable to need it.'

CHAPTER SEVEN

Dropping out of the hills south of Skyline Ridge, Beauregarde glimpsed Skillet's lights against the deep and moonless gloom. It was a feeble flicker at that distance, but it stirred a quick lift of eagerness in him—a rush and savage eagerness that pushed him like a prodding hand. For that small beacon marked the end of long and stubborn searching; it beckoned him to the final showdown.

Beauregarde urged his horse to a faster pace. The animal quartered into a trail's hoof-worn trough which Beauregarde identified as the trail he had followed on his other night ride to the Skillet. Recalling the incidents of that visit, he cursed himself for not solving the simple riddle of Strebor's name; he had been close enough to touch Roberts that night . . .

Dust smell registered in Beauregarde's nostrils, and that thin taint turned him instantly vigilant. Checking his horse, he keened the night air for sound of travel. None came, but because he knew the hock-deep dust of this trail would muffle hoof tromps to a minimum, Beauregarde halted. The odor of freshly risen dust could mean but one thing—someone had passed that way within a matter of minutes.

Wondering if that rider had been traveling north or south, Beauregarde dismounted. He struck a match, and saw fresh hoof prints in the dust. Those tracks were headed south, showing the wide spread of a hard-running horse. And they were so recently made that tiny particles of rimming sand were still slowly settling into the pocks.

Who, he asked himself, could this rider ahead of him be? And why was he traveling at so urgent a pace? If there'd been several sets of tracks, Beauregarde would have guessed at some last-minute change in Dave Blake's plans, would have decided that Tate Corvette's impatience had hastened the raid on the Skillet. But there was only one set of tracks—one rider rushing toward the Skillet.

The puzzle of that kept nagging at Beauregarde's mind as he rode southward.

What possible reason could there be for that man's presence out there ahead of him? If Hank Lundermann was alive, there'd be no puzzle at all; the solution would be simple. And even though Lundermann was permanently removed from further spying, Beauregarde could turn up no other reason for fast travel on that trail tonight. Someone was intending to warn Strebor. But who?

Abruptly then Beauregarde's mind caught at a fresh possibility. Supposing all the evidence against Lundermann was false and the big cowman hadn't been Strebor's spy? Suppose someone else had played the Judas role?

Deliberately reviewing all the evidence, Beauregarde reached the negative conclusion that though it seemed to point directly at Lundermann, the evidence was still guesswork—a matter of hunch and conjecture. Whereupon he turned his thinking to a calculation of the proposition that Lundermann hadn't been the Judas; that Blake had been sold out by someone else entirely. He made a mental lineup of men, and excluding only Dave Blake and himself, gave each a probing consideration. Oscar Ellison, he decided at once, was out of it. No man whose home had been burned and whose wife had been subjected to last night's travail would be riding now to warn Sid Strebor. Cliff Paddock he also discarded as a suspect

194

on two counts—the burn-out at Boxed P, and Paddock's courtship of Susan. Jeb Hodnett? Well, the man would have to be an arch scoundrel and a brilliant actor combined; he seemed honest as a steeldust horse. The same was true of Tate Corvette, with the additional circumstance of young Pike's serious condition boosting the tally against Corvette being in cahoots with Strebor.

No, Beauregarde decided, none of these men . . .

Sam Derbyshire!

Could it be that Derbyshire wasn't the blundering old lawdog he'd seemed? Had Derbyshire played a crafty game against Blake on the pretext of wanting peace at any price? It seemed highly improbable, almost ridiculous. Yet ridiculous or not, *someone* was out there riding hell-bent for the Skillet.

Remembering that Derbyshire had exposed Strebor's true identity by handing him Red Valentine's letter, Beauregarde shrugged away the thought that Sheriff Sam was implicated in any way. Hell, the man wouldn't have shown him that letter if he was Strebor's tool.

Yet a moment later the grasping talons of Beauregarde's mind snatched at a fresh possibility. Supposing Derbyshire had revealed Strebor's true identity with deliberate intent to lure him into a slaughter trap at the

Skillet? If Strebor and Derbyshire were working together, the sheriff might well know his swarthy employer's real name, and already knowing that Beauregarde was looking for a man named Roberts, would have taken this opportunity to send him into a prepared trap . . .

All this, Beauregarde realized, was against every indication of Derbyshire's character. It seemed too far-fetched; too completely at variance with the man's easy-going, prideful ways. Sam Derbyshire had shown no slightest sign of being capable of such treachery. Yet *someone* had played the Judas role, and was playing it again tonight!

The thorough conviction that this was so—that the rider ahead of him was Strebor's spy—brought a quick caution to Lee Beauregarde. It banked the fire of his impatience, caused him to halt his horse some two miles north of the Skillet's lamplight. If his calculations were correct, the deep arroyo he had used before ran a crescent-shaped course a trifle west of where he now stood. And if his suspicion of Derbyshire should prove correct, he would need to use considerable judgment in approaching the Skillet.

Fear of death or bodily mishap played no motivating part in these cautious calculations. Beauregarde had faced death on numerous occasions without fear of consequence. But there was another kind of fear in him now; an almost frantic fear of missing what might be his one and only chance to pay the debt he owed Sid Strebor—or rather, Sid Roberts. This was the thing he'd waited for; the thing to which his gun had been dedicated three long years before. It had dominated his thinking; had warped his mind and made him older than his years.

Now, after all the futile searching he had found Roberts. And because dead men do not pay debts, he had to stay alive—had to guard his hate; had to nourish and protect it for a full payment.

Reaching the arroyo, Beauregarde rode into it. He had intended to follow the defile as a precautionary measure, but it was too narrow there, and so he climbed up the opposite bank and rode toward the Skillet at an angle which would bring him to the house from its west side.

The ground was sandy there, and he sent his horse forward at a shuffling trot. But later, arriving at the packed earth of the yard, he approached the juniper pole corral at a walk. Dismounting there, he hitched his horse to a fence post and removed his spurs. Then, nudging his gun loose in its leather, he walked past the bunkhouse, which was dark, and apparently deserted.

A saddle horse, standing in front of the

house, made a looming shadow against the doorway's faint illumination. Skirting the windmill and a wagonshed, Beauregarde went quickly across a window's shaft of light and, reaching the veranda, stepped up. There he halted, and had the queerly startling sensation of being watched by someone behind him. Whirling instantly, he probed the yard's farther darkness without finding anything. Yet the premonition of a presence behind him didn't dissolve. It increased.

Long riding on lonely trails had sharpened Beauregarde's perceptions. Even though there were voices inside the house, and no sound nor sign of movement in the yard, he sensed there was someone between him and the darkened bunkhouse. It was an intangible thing, this presentiment; unseen and unheard, yet so strongly real it held him in strict, unmoving silence for a moment longer.

And during that interval of taut listening, Sid Strebor's voice drifted out to him—an angry, accusing voice . . .

'It should've been easy for you to cut down that trail crew when the shooting started. Why in hell didn't you?'

There was a brief pause, and in this momentary silence, it occurred to Beauregarde that here was the answer to the riddle which had plagued him so long. The rider in there with Strebor would be the man who'd framed the brand blotching job on Oscar Ellison; the man who'd tipped Strebor to the beef drive!

And that man wasn't Hank Lundermann . . .

A second voice, low and hesitating, said, 'That wasn't part of the bargain, Sid.'

Something about that second voice tinkled a bell in Beauregarde's brain. The voice seemed familiar, yet it didn't sound like Sam Derbyshire's voice . . .

Then it came again, louder—more distinct. 'The raid on Three Links wasn't in our bargain either, Sid.'

Abruptly then, and for the second time that night, utter astonishment smashed through Lee Beauregarde. *That voice belonged to Cliff Paddock!*

Amazement churned Beauregarde's thoughts into a welter of confusion. It drove all thought of that yonderly stalking presence from his mind; it turned him toward the doorway in a spasmodic move to obtain visual proof of what his ears had told him. The revelation that Sid Strebor was the man he'd sought so long had been a tremendous surprise; but this was somehow more monstrous—more shocking. It was almost beyond belief!

Going quietly along the veranda, Beauregarde listened to the conversation of those inside voices.

'Why didn't you tell me you were sending Valentine and Savoy to raid the house?'

Paddock demanded resentfully.

'Because I knew how goddam sweet you was on Blake's girl,' Strebor snapped. 'And because I knew something else, Paddock—I knew you'd sell out if you ever got the chance. Well, you ain't going to get the chance!'

Beauregarde reached the doorway, saw the two men facing each other across a littered table—and saw the gun in Sid Strebor's hand. They made a dramatic tableau; a strangely violent tableau despite their postured stillness. Paddock stood rigidly straight with perspiration greasing his rugged, lamplit face. His right hand was half raised, and sight of the cameo ring on its little finger brought another startling disclosure to Lee Beauregarde . . .

Recalling the bluish thread caught under a claw of that ring the day he'd met Paddock in the hills, Beauregarde knew now why the color of that brand-blotched grulla steer had afterward seemed important. The bluish thread hadn't been a thread at all; it had been a hair snagged from the grulla while Paddock was working the brand!

No wonder Sam Derbyshire had been so sure Skillet riders hadn't tampered with the brand. There'd been no fresh southerly tracks because Cliff Paddock had ridden northward upon completion of his treacherous task. The burning of the Boxed P shack, Beauregarde decided, had been just a clever gesture to ward off any possibility of suspicion against Paddock.

All this Beauregarde realized in the fleeting interval while Sid Strebor stood crouched and darkly scowling, with killer glint showing brighter and brighter in his black eyes.

'Once a sneak, always a sneak,' Strebor said contemptuously. 'I brought you into this country because I needed an ace in the hole. But you turned out to be a goddam deuce—a skirt-chasing deuce of hearts!'

Paddock took that accusation in stiff silence, but when Strebor said, 'You'd sell out your own brother for a fancy woman's smile,' Paddock blurted, 'No, Sid—I never meant to sell you out! Honest I didn't!'

'You're a stinking liar,' Strebor snarled, plainly goading himself into a rage. 'You just told me Beauregarde killed Red, but you were lying, damn you. Ace-High heard the right story—how Red had Beauregarde all stacked for chopping when you drilled him in the back. And that's the way I'll give it to you, Paddock, if you'll turn around!'

*　　*　　*

Cliff Paddock's face went chalky gray. He said, 'There's still a chance to clean up big in this country, Sid. You and Gregg ride out for a spell and wait till things cool off. And next time we'll do it right. I'll go all the way with you, Sid—all the way!'

'Like hell you will!' Strebor snapped. 'There ain't going to be no next time, my friend. Not for you. And you ain't going no place except hell!'

He waggled the leveled gun and asked tauntingly, 'You want to make a grab, Paddock? Or do you want it cold-turkey?'

Watching this, Beauregarde saw Paddock's shoulder muscles tighten. He thought the Boxed P owner was going to make his play. That was what Beauregarde was waiting for, and wanting. Paddock wouldn't have a chance, but he could at least die like a man. Even though Paddock had been a dirty, double-crossing Judas all these months while courting Susan, he might be man enough to make a grab . . .

But Paddock's right hand didn't move. His burly shoulders slumped as if weighted by a burden he couldn't bear, and stark fear washed the last remnant of pride from his staring eyes.

'Don't shoot!' he pleaded in a voice gone high and quavering. 'For God's sake don't shoot!'

Strebor laughed—a mirthless, mocking, sardonic laugh. 'Too bad Red ain't here to see this,' he chuckled. 'By God, Red would've enjoyed it!'

He thumbed back the gun's hammer, and

the mechanical click sounded loud and ominous. And in that instant it occurred to Lee Beauregarde that he had two debts to pay here instead of one—that because Cliff Paddock had saved his life the night before he must save Paddock now. Even though Paddock deserved to die, he couldn't see him slaughtered in cold blood—and that was the way it was going to be.

Whereupon Beauregarde drew his gun, stepped into the doorway and said sharply, 'Roberts!'

That single word seemed to freeze the Skillet's boss. For one taut moment he stood stiffly unmoving. He didn't turn his head, nor shift his glance, nor seem to breathe. Time stretched out, the seconds trooping long and slow, like caterpillars crawling on parade.

It was a nerve-racking thing, this silence. A nagging thing. It gnawed at a man's mind and greased the palms of his hands with perspiration. There was nothing new about it to Beauregarde; it was the same familiar scene, with death waiting so close it had a feel and smell to it.

And because his need for vengeance was like a rearing monster inside him, Beauregarde tried to drive himself to the same merciless, cold-turkey killing which Strebor had just threatened; tried to lift his thumb from the hammer of his leveled gun. It would need to move only a fraction of an inch, that thumb. But because Strebor's gun was still pointed at Paddock and Strebor wasn't even looking in this direction, Beauregarde couldn't force himself to fire . . .

Seeing this as a weakness in himself, and wholly resenting it, Beauregarde said savagely, 'All right, Roberts—leather your smokepole and we'll start over.'

That command seemed to startle the Skillet's boss. He stood unmoving for a moment longer; then slowly sheathed his gun and turned to face Beauregarde with a look of profound puzzlement in his brittle black eyes.

Beauregarde slid his gun into its holster and said flatly, 'You didn't give my father much of a chance, Roberts. Which is about what I'm giving you now. I'll beat you by three bullets and then throw my gun at you, Roberts. Grab your gun!'

A crafty light flashed into Strebor's sharply inquisitive eyes. And in this instant, as the sound of stealthy footsteps registered in Beauregarde's ears, Ace-High Gregg snarled, 'Hold it, Texican—hold it!'

Sid Strebor's swarthy features relaxed into an expansive smile. He glanced at Paddock, who stood rigidly watching, then laughed gloatingly at Beauregarde. 'You been gigging your rowels real high, saddle bum. You been sunning your damn belly all over and yonderly like a rough-string bronc bucking off all comers. But beginning right now you're buzzard bait, Beauregarde—just buzzard bait!'

Strebor drew his gun, the weapon seemed large in his slender womanish hand. Beauregarde couldn't see Ace-High Gregg, but he could hear the fat rider's heavy breathing and so guessed that Gregg wasn't more than three or four feet behind him. There'd be no chance to beat out both these guns; even though Strebor hadn't yet raised his, Gregg's gun would be aimed and cocked—ready for instant firing. No, there wasn't a chance there. Not the slightest shadow of a chance. This was the inevitable end, the futile finale for a six-gun smokeroo when his luck had run out.

Strebor waggled him down-tilted gun and chuckled amusedly. 'You don't talk so much,' he said tauntingly. 'But your friend Paddock has talked a lot. He says the Pool bunch are coming down here to hang me and Gregg; that they're meeting at Skyline Spring.'

Beauregarde glanced at Paddock and silently cursed him. The witless attempt to save this double-crossing informer had already cost him his revenge. In a minute now it would also cost him his life . . .

Paddock met Beauregarde's gaze for a split second; then his eyes shifted in a swift glance at Gregg. There was something queer about that—something that kindled a spark of speculation in Beauregarde's brain. But Strebor's gloating voice disrupted that half-formed curiosity.

'There won't be no hangings tonight, saddle bum. But there'll be plenty shooting up at Skyline Spring along about three o'clock in the morning. Mebbe me and Gregg will cut down the whole goddam caboodle, eh, Gregg?'

The fat rider behind Beauregarde loosed a dribbling laugh. 'Sure we will, and it'll be a cinch,' he agreed. 'We'll have 'em bunched in one bundle, boss. We'll chop 'em down like pigs in a pen.'

So that was why Strebor was so jubilant!

It wasn't just because of this deal here—this surething slaughter of a disobedient spy and the son of a marshal he'd murdered in Texas. It was more than that—much more. It was the exultation of a thoroughly rapacious man; the ghoulish glee of a rangehog anticipating ultimate success for his scheme of greedy conquest . . .

The enormity of it sent a sleeting coldness through Beauregarde's veins. Because of Paddock's treachery, and his own carelessness, this calculating killer was going to grasp victory from the very ashes of defeat. Dave Blake and his friends would be blasted into oblivion. Young Oscar Ellison, who'd named his first born son after a renegade Texican, would die; Tate Corvette, Jeb Hodnett, Sam

Derbyshire—all of them would die.

Then abruptly Beauregarde stomped down the feeling of utter futility which had momentarily gripped him. Here was something bigger, something infinitely more urgent than revenge. A thing so important that even a dying man must attempt it. There was no chance for a survival here, but there might be a chance to save good men from slaughter. Just a sleazy, shadowy ghost of a chance, yet one well worth the taking!

A devil-be-damned grin quirked Lee Beauregarde's lips. He said, 'I came here to kill you,' and glimpsed swift astonishment in Strebor's eyes. Then he snapped, 'I'm doing it, Roberts—right now!'

As he spoke the last word Beauregarde dropped to his knees, a split second before Gregg's gun exploded. And in that same instant, while Beauregarde made the fastest draw of his gun-smoked career, he saw Sid Strebor's swarthy face above the blurred barrel of a swiftly shifting gun.

Those two weapons blasted simultaneously. But Lee Beauregarde didn't hear them. He scarcely felt the plucking lash of a slug that sliced the flesh along his ribs, nor was he aware of the way his gun continued to buck against his palm. All his senses at this moment were centered in one overwhelming emotion—in the tumultuous release of his festering hatred for Sid Roberts, an emotion so fiercely fundamental that even the expected smash of a bullet in his back didn't diminish his high exultation. Brutally, savagely, Beauregarde fired at the smoke-hazed form that reeled in grotesque retreat before him. He fired again and again, until his gun was empty—until the murderer of Marshal Jeff Beauregarde sprawled lifeless on the blood-spattered floor.

Then, and only then, was Beauregarde aware of the astonishing fact that though there'd been other gun blasts in this room, no slug had smashed into his back. Dazedly, as a man not sure of his senses, Beauregarde got to his feet.

Cliff Paddock stood leaning indolently against the room's front wall, a smoking gun held out in front of him. All the frozen rigidity was gone from Paddock's face now; the old rash smile was on his lips and his voice held its familiar drawl when he said, 'You shouldn't've have emptied your gun into Strebor. You and Sid weren't exactly alone, you know.'

That didn't quite make sense to Beauregarde. Not at first. He glanced toward the doorway and saw that Ace-High Gregg was dead. Paddock, he thought then, was taking this way of saying he'd saved him from a bullet in the back . . .

But when Beauregarde glanced at Paddock again he knew that wasn't what he meant. For Paddock still held the smoking gun, and he was taking deliberate aim!

'Too bad it has to be this way,' Paddock drawled.

The smile had gone crooked now, and he stood crouched. Even his voice had changed; there was a peculiar thickness in it.

'What,' Beauregarde inquired, 'do you mean it's too bad?'

Paddock drew in a long breath, like a man preparing for a plunge into cold water. 'It's too bad you got to die,' he muttered. 'But you know too damned much, Texican. And you like Susan too damned well. If you told her what you heard here tonight I'd lose her sure. And I'd have to leave the country, which same I don't hanker to do. So I got to fix it so's you won't tell her, Texican.'

Beauregarde's fingers gripped his empty gun. He watched Cliff Paddock prime himself for murder—and was tensing his muscles for a desperate, lastditch leap at that wall-propped form when he saw Paddock's gun hand waver. And in that same instant, as Beauregarde glimpsed blood seeping through Paddock's shirt front, he understood why the blocky rider was standing propped against the wall. Paddock was wounded. He had killed Gregg—but not before one of Gregg's bullets had found its mark!

Even as that astounding realization came to him, Beauregarde saw death drape its ghostly pallor across Paddock's face. Paddock's hand sagged lower and lower, as if the gun it held was too heavy a burden. He made a feeble attempt to tilt it up; then his body slid slowly down the wall. For a brief, suspended moment, Paddock sat there with a foolish grin on his slack-jawed face. He tried to tilt up the gun again; he was still trying when he tipped over sideways and lay loosely unmoving.

Beauregarde's held breath ran out of him in a gusty sigh. His luck, he reflected, had come close to running out there tonight. And it was hugely ironical that his survival had been accomplished by two men who had intended to kill him. Only Cliff Paddock's unanticipated play against Gregg could have saved him from a bullet in the back while he was killing Sid Roberts. And, except for Gregg's slug, Paddock would have killed him in cold blood . . .

Presently then, Beauregarde lifted a tarnished law badge from his coat pocket, and, absently polishing the star against his shirt, said, 'Took a long time, Dad. A hell of a long time. But Roberts got his needin's.'

★   ★   ★

Lee Beauregarde rode into Apache Tank shortly after midnight and, dismounting at the livery, turned his horse over to Joe Fagan.

The little liveryman eyed the saddle-tied warbag and asked, 'You ain't fixin' to leave us, be you?'

'Yeah,' Beauregarde muttered. 'I'm heading back to Texas.'

'That's too bad,' Fagan exclaimed regretfully. 'I thought mebbe you'd settle down here in the valley.'

Then he asked, 'Say—ain't you goin' to be in on the big wind-up at the Skillet in the mornin'?'

Beauregarde shook his head, whereat Fagan said, 'Me and two three others is meetin' the Pool bunch at Skyline Spring. We're agoin' to give Sid Strebor a surprise he won't live to remember.'

Beauregarde smiled thinly. There'd be a surprise at the Skillet all right, a big surprise. But it would be Dave Blake and his friends who'd get it. He said, 'Guess I'll get a drink before the saloon closes.'

'We won't be leavin' for a few minutes yet,' Fagan said. 'Come on with us and have some fun.'

'No,' Beauregarde muttered, and went on out to the sidewalk. 'I've had fun enough to last me for quite a spell.'

Walking toward the Senate Saloon, he wondered what Dave Blake would think when the cowman found Paddock's body with Strebor's and Gregg's at the Skillet. Blake, he guessed, would think Paddock had decided to pull a one-man attack, and had been killed in a shoot-out battle.

And how would Susan feel about Paddock's death?

These were the questions Beauregarde considered as he sat down to drink at a table in the Senate. It occurred to him that he could stay over until tomorrow and tell his story to Susan; could probably convince her that Paddock had been in cahoots with Strebor all along. But it would be a difficult thing to do, and he had no way of proving his fantastic story. Recalling how utterly astonished he'd been upon hearing Paddock's voice at the Skillet, Beauregarde shrugged wearily. It was an ironical situation. Alive or dead, Cliff Paddock seemed destined to spoil every chance another man might have with Susan. Even though she might be willing to believe the story, she'd naturally be skeptical about the manner of Paddock's dying. She'd be wondering why a six-gun smokeroo should shy away from an opportunity to eliminate a rival, especially when he knew that rival was a double-crossing coyote who needed killing. It didn't sound quite reasonable, and whatever doubt the story left with Susan would always be a barrier between them.

No, he decided, there was no good reason for his staying overnight in Apache Tank.

Better to have a few fine memories unspoiled by bitterness; better to remember Susan as he'd last seen her, smiling down at him in the bunkhouse. Or better yet, the way she had lain in his arms up there in the piney woods. That was how he'd best remember her . . .

Beauregarde drained his glass in the eager fashion of a man seeking solace in drunken oblivion. He was pouring a second drink when Honest John came over and eyed him thoughtfully.

'You figgerin' to spend the night here?' the saloonman inquired.

Beauregarde contemplated the bottle in front of him. 'No,' he said. 'Just long enough to finish this. Mebbe half an hour or so. I don't like to hurry my drinking.'

Ogden consulted the clock above the bare. 'It's way past my closin' time,' he announced. 'I'm takin' a little pasear with Joe Fagan.'

'So?' Beauregarde mused, not bothering to glance up. 'Well, I bought this whiskey here and I calculate to drink it here.'

Honest John held up a pudgy hand and said quickly, 'All right, friend. All right. Stay long as you like, but do me the favor of snapping the padlock on the door when you go out. You've got the whole shebang all to yourself.'

He went on out then, and Beauregarde said musingly, 'The whole shebang.'

Afterward the hoof-pound of departing

213

horses drifted back along the street, that broken beat of sound soon fading. Silence settled down on this long sour-smelling room, giving it a dismal air of emptiness . . .

Beauregarde shivered. There was a coldness in him which the whiskey hadn't touched, a coldness and a queer feeling of indecision. For the first time in three years there was no goal ahead of him, no scourge of hatred to push him on along the trail. All the urgent need for vengeance had flowed out of him in that brief moment of blasting guns at Skillet; now he was entirely stranded, without purpose or plan.

He poured a drink and, gulping the whiskey down, waited for it to thaw the cold knot at the pit of his stomach. And in that interval of moody waiting, Beauregarde reviewed the curious happenings since the first night he'd sat in the saloon. He hadn't known Susan that night; he hadn't held her in his arms, hadn't felt the intimate pressure of her body against him, nor tasted the sweet flavor of her lips. There'd been no romantic notions in him that night; he'd just been a tough young trail tramp with a grudge against the whole damned world. But now there was no toughness in him; just a sort of dismal emptiness.

It occurred to him then that no amount of whiskey could thaw the coldness in him—that this guzzling was entirely futile. Thoroughly disgusted, he knocked the bottle from the table with a clubbing blow, got up and stood scowling at the spilled liquor which formed a pool upon the floor. Then he walked to the stoop and, slamming the door behind him, snapped the padlock.

The thought came to him that he was locking more than a saloon here tonight. He was locking up his first high hope of romance—and his last. But there was no way of putting a padlock on his thoughts. Regret would ride with him from this town; it would be his haunting companion on every trail he ever rode.

Beauregarde was savoring the full bitterness of that realization when he turned into the livery's lantern-lit doorway and saw Susan sitting on Joe Fagan's rawhide chair.

For a moment of absolute incredulity he thought he was drunk—drunker than he'd ever been. He thought the whiskey had turned him completely loco. But when Susan stood up he knew this was no drunkard's dream. She was there, standing so close he could reach out and touch her!

She didn't smile, and for a long moment she didn't speak. The ride from Three Links had put a rosy tint on her cheeks; her eyes were brightly shining in the lantern's reflected light, and her slim, gloved hands were clasped tightly between the twin mounds of her high breasts. There was an air of eagerness and

215

expectancy about her, but when she spoke her voice held a note of reserve which puzzled Beauregarde.

'I met John Ogden back on the road,' she explained, her eyes continuing to study his gaunt beard-bristled face as if searching for something she couldn't find. 'Honest John said you were staging a one-man spree.'

Then she added with quiet humor, 'It didn't seem quite proper for me to go into the Senate, so I waited for you here.'

Some of the coldness ran out of Beauregarde then. The thought flashed sharply through his confused mind that this girl didn't know Cliff Paddock was dead. She couldn't know. Yet she had ridden all the way from Three Links to sit there and wait for a six-gun smokeroo. That must mean something; it must mean that Paddock's hero play hadn't changed her feelings toward him after all!

The fast-forming conviction that this was so held Beauregarde speechless. He tried to recall the exact words which had made him so sure she'd gone back to Paddock . . .

She said censuringly, 'You shouldn't have left without saying goodbye, Lee. I didn't know you'd taken your warbag with you until Orphelia Corvette told me. What made you decide to leave so suddenly?'

Beauregarde's fatigue-honed features eased into a self-mocking grin. 'I never was a very

216

good loser,' he admitted, 'and I thought I'd lost you. Mebbe I put a wrong meaning to what you said in the bunkhouse, but I was sure you'd decided Paddock was the man you wanted to marry, or at least the man you felt you had to marry!'

'So that was it!' she exclaimed, and her hands came out to grip his arms.

She was smiling now, all the reserve was gone from her voice, and in that moment she was again the frankly emotional girl he'd held in his arms up in the piney woods. She said, 'I thought your interest in Judy Lundermann's safety meant that you preferred her to me. I thought she had vamped you way from me as she'd often tried to vamp Cliff. How could we have misunderstood each other so greatly, my dear?'

The last loop of the cold knot dissolved in Lee Beauregarde. His good right arm went around Susan's shoulders and he stood for a moment savoring the shadowed sweetness of her upturned face, seeing all the things a man wants to see in a woman. Until presently he thought of the way Cliff Paddock had died, and that sobered him instantly. Even though Susan hadn't chosen Paddock, she might not want to marry the man who'd killed him—and there was no way he could prove he hadn't killed Cliff Paddock.

He said slowly, searching for the proper

words, 'There's something I've got to t
you. Something you'll have to believe witho
proof.'

He watched her closely, expecting to s
some change in her expression, and dreadi
to see it. But there was none. Her li
remained parted in their sweet-curving smi
and she murmured softly, 'If I needed pro
of anything I wouldn't be here, Lee. I'd l
home—sobbing my heart out for a tall Texic
who'd gone away without saying goodbye.'

Which was when Lee Beauregarde kisse
her in the rashly possessive way of a ma
claiming his heart's desire . . .